Absen

ALSO BY 'MARY WESTMACOTT'

The Burden
A Daughter's a Daughter
Giant's Bread
The Rose and the Yew Tree
Unfinished Portrait

ALSO AVAILABLE BY
'AGATHA CHRISTIE MALLOWAN'

Come, Tell Me How You Live
Star Over Bethlehem

AGATHA CHRISTIE
WRITING AS
MARY WESTMACOTT

Absent in the Spring

HarperCollins*Publishers*

HarperCollins*Publishers*
77–85 Fulham Palace Road,
Hammersmith, London W6 8JB

This paperback edition 1997
1 3 5 7 9 8 6 4 2

Previously published in paperback by Fontana 1973
First published 1944

ISBN 0 00 649947 3

Set in Sabon by
Rowland Phototypesetting Ltd,
Bury St Edmunds, Suffolk

Printed and bound in Great Britain by
Caledonian International Book Manufacturing Ltd, Glasgow

From you have I been absent in the Spring . . .

Chapter One

Joan Scudamore screwed up her eyes as she peered across the dimness of the rest house dining-room. She was slightly short-sighted.

Surely that's – no it isn't – I believe it *is*. Blanche Haggard.

Extraordinary – right out in the wilds – to come across an old school friend whom she hadn't seen for – oh quite fifteen years.

At first, Joan was delighted by the discovery. She was by nature a sociable woman, always pleased to run across friends and acquaintances.

She thought to herself, But, poor dear, how dreadfully she's changed. She looks years older. Literally *years*. After all, she can't be more than – what, forty-eight?

It was a natural sequence after that to glance at her own appearance in the mirror that happened, most conveniently, to hang just beside the table. What she saw there put her in an even better humour.

Really, thought Joan Scudamore, I've worn very well.

She saw a slender, middle-aged woman with a singularly unlined face, brown hair hardly touched with grey, pleasant blue eyes and a cheerful smiling mouth. The woman was dressed in a neat, cool travelling coat and skirt and carried a rather large bag containing the necessities of travel.

Joan Scudamore was travelling back from Baghdad to London by the overland route. She had come up by the train from Baghdad last night. She was to sleep in the railway rest house tonight and go on by car tomorrow morning.

It was the sudden illness of her younger daughter that had brought her post haste out from England, her realization of William's (her son-in-law) impracticability, and of the chaos that would arise in a household without efficient control.

Well, that was all right now. She had taken charge, made arrangements. The baby, William, Barbara convalescent, everything had been planned and set in good running order. Thank goodness, thought Joan, I've always had a head on my shoulders.

William and Barbara had been full of gratitude. They'd pressed her to stay on, not to rush back, but she had smilingly, albeit with a stifled sigh, refused. For there was Rodney to consider – poor old Rodney stuck in Crayminster, up to his ears in work and with no one in the house to look after his comfort except servants.

'And after all,' said Joan, 'what are servants?'

Barbara said:

'*Your* servants, Mother, are always perfection. You see to that!'

She had laughed, but she had been pleased all the same. Because when all was said and done one did like appreciation. She had sometimes wondered if her family took a little too much for granted the smooth running of the house and her own care and devotion.

Not really that she had any criticism to make. Tony, Averil and Barbara were delightful children and she and Rodney had every reason to be proud of their upbringing and of their success in life.

Tony was growing oranges out in Rhodesia, Averil, after giving her parents some momentary anxiety, had settled down as the wife of a wealthy and charming stockbroker. Barbara's husband had a good job in the Public Works Department in Iraq.

They were all nice-looking healthy children with pleasant manners. Joan felt that she and Rodney were indeed fortunate – and privately she was of the opinion that some of the credit was to be ascribed to them as parents. After all, they had brought the children up very carefully, taking infinite pains over the choice of nurses and governesses, and later of schools and always putting the welfare and well-being of the children first.

Joan felt a little gentle glow as she turned away from her image in the glass. She thought, Well, it's nice to feel one's been a success at one's job. I never wanted a career, or anything of that kind. I was quite content to be a wife and mother. I married the man I loved, and he's been a success at his job – and perhaps that's owing to me a bit too. One can do so much by influence. Dear Rodney!

And her heart warmed to the thought that soon, very soon, she would be seeing Rodney again. She'd never been away from him for very long before. What a happy peaceful life they had had together.

Well, perhaps *peaceful* was rather overstating it. Family life was never quite peaceful. Holidays, infectious illnesses, broken pipes in winter. Life really was a series of petty dramas. And Rodney had always worked very hard, harder perhaps than was good for his health. He'd been badly run down that time six years ago. He hadn't, Joan thought with compunction, worn quite as well as she had. He stooped rather, and there was a lot of white in his hair. He had a tired look, too, about the eyes.

Still, after all, that was life. And now, with the children married, and the firm doing so well, and the new partner bringing fresh money in, Rodney could take things more easily. He and she would have time to enjoy themselves. They must entertain more – have a week or two in London every now and then. Rodney, perhaps, might take up golf.

Yes, really she couldn't think why she hadn't persuaded him to take up golf before. So healthy, especially when he had to do so much office work.

Having settled that point in her mind, Mrs Scudamore looked across the dining-room once more at the woman whom she believed to be her former school friend.

Blanche Haggard. How she had adored Blanche Haggard when they were at St Anne's together! Everyone was crazy about Blanche. She had been so daring, so amusing, and yes, so absolutely *lovely*. Funny to think of that now, looking at that thin, restless, untidy elderly woman. What extraordinary clothes! And she looked – really she looked – at least sixty . . .

Of course, thought Joan, she's had a very unfortunate life.

A momentary impatience rose in her. The whole thing seemed such a wanton waste. There was Blanche, twenty-one, with the world at her feet – looks, position, everything – and she had had to throw in her lot with that quite unspeakable man. A vet – yes, actually a *vet*. A vet with a wife, too, which made it worse. Her people had behaved with commendable firmness, taking her round the world on one of those pleasure cruises. And Blanche had actually got off the boat somewhere, Algiers, or Naples, and come home and joined her vet. And naturally he had lost his practice, and started drinking, and his wife hadn't wished to divorce him. Presently they'd left Crayminster and after that Joan hadn't heard anything of Blanche for years, not until she'd run across her one day in London at Harrods where they had met in the shoe department, and after a little discreet conversation (discreet on Joan's part, Blanche had never set any store by discretion) she had discovered that Blanche was now married to a man called Holliday who was in an insurance office, but Blanche thought he was going to resign soon because he wanted to write a book about Warren

Hastings and he wanted to give all his time to it, not just write scraps when he came back from the office.

Joan had murmured that in that case she supposed he had private means? And Blanche had replied cheerfully that he hadn't got a cent! Joan had said that perhaps to give up his job would be rather unwise, unless he was sure the book would be a success. Was it commissioned? Oh dear me, no, said Blanche cheerfully, and as a matter of fact she didn't really think the book would be a success, because though Tom was very keen on it, he really didn't write very well. Whereupon Joan had said with some warmth that Blanche must put her foot down, to which Blanche had responded with a stare and a 'But he wants to write, the poor pet. He wants it more than anything.' Sometimes, Joan said, one had to be wise for two. Blanche had laughed and remarked that she herself had never even been wise enough for one!

Thinking that over, Joan felt that it was only too unfortunately true. A year later she saw Blanche in a restaurant with a peculiar, flashy looking woman and two flamboyantly artistic men. After that the only reminder she had had of Blanche's existence was five years later when Blanche wrote and asked for a loan of fifty pounds. Her little boy, she said, needed an operation. Joan had sent her twenty-five and a kind letter asking for details. The response was a postcard with scrawled on it: *Good for you, Joan. I knew you wouldn't let me down* – which was gratifying in a way, but hardly satisfactory. After that, silence. And now here, in a Near Eastern railway rest house, with kerosene lamps flaring and spluttering amidst a smell of rancid mutton fat and paraffin and Flit, was the friend of so many years ago, incredibly aged and coarsened and the worse for wear.

Blanche finished her dinner first and was on her way out when she caught sight of the other. She stopped dead.

'Holy Moses, it's Joan!'

A moment or two later she had pulled up her chair to the table and the two were chatting together.

Presently Blanche said:

'Well, *you've* worn well, my dear. You look about thirty. Where have you been all these years? In cold storage?'

'Hardly that. I've been in Crayminster.'

'Born, bred, married and buried in Crayminster,' said Blanche.

Joan said with a laugh:

'Is that so bad a fate?'

Blanche shook her head.

'No,' she said seriously. 'I'd say it was a pretty good one. What's happened to your children? You had some children, didn't you?'

'Yes, three. A boy and two girls. The boy is in Rhodesia. The girls are married. One lives in London. I've just been visiting the other one out in Baghdad. Her name is Wray – Barbara Wray.'

Blanche nodded.

'I've seen her. Nice kid. Married rather too young, didn't she?'

'I don't think so,' said Joan stiffly. 'We all like William very much, and they are happy together.'

'Yes, they seem to be settling down all right now. The baby has probably been a settling influence. Having a child does sort of steady a girl down. Not,' added Blanche thoughtfully, 'that it ever steadied me. I was very fond of those two kids of mine – Len and Mary. And yet when Johnnie Pelham came along, I went off with him and left them behind without a second thought.'

Joan looked at her with disapprobation.

'Really, Blanche,' she said warmly. 'How could you?'

'Rotten of me, wasn't it?' said Blanche. 'Of course I knew they'd be all right with Tom. He always adored them. He married a really nice domestic girl. Suited him far better than I ever did. She saw that he had decent meals and mended his underclothes and all that. Dear Tom, he was always a pet. He used to send me a card at Christmas and Easter for years afterwards which was nice of him, don't you think?'

Joan did not answer. She was too full of conflicting thoughts. The predominant one was wonder that this – *this* – could be Blanche Haggard – that well-bred, high-spirited girl who had been the star pupil at St Anne's. This really slatternly woman with apparently no shame in revealing the more sordid details of her life, and in such common language too! Why, Blanche Haggard had won the prize for English at St Anne's!

Blanche reverted to a former topic.

'Fancy little Barbara Wray being your daughter, Joan. That just shows how people get things wrong. Everyone had got it into their heads that she was so unhappy at home that she'd married the first man who asked her in order to escape.'

'How ridiculous. Where do these stories come from?'

'I can't imagine. Because I'm pretty sure of one thing, Joan and that is that you've always been an admirable mother. I can't imagine you being cross or unkind.'

'That's nice of you, Blanche. I think I may say that we've always given our children a very happy home and done everything possible for their happiness. I think it's so important, you know, that one should be *friends* with one's children.'

'Very nice – if one ever can.'

'Oh, I think you can. It's just a question of remembering your own youth and putting yourself in their place.' Joan's charming, serious face was bent a little nearer to that of her former friend. 'Rodney and I have always tried to do that.'

'Rodney? Let me see, you married a solicitor, didn't you? Of course – I went to their firm at the time when

Harry was trying to get a divorce from that awful wife of his. I believe it was your husband we saw – Rodney Scudamore. He was extraordinarily nice and kind, most understanding. And you've stayed put with him all these years. No fresh deals?'

Joan said rather stiffly:

'Neither of us have wanted a fresh deal. Rodney and I have been perfectly contented with one another.'

'Of course you always were as cold as a fish, Joan. But I should have said that husband of yours had quite a roving eye!'

'Really, Blanche!'

Joan flushed angrily. A roving eye, indeed. Rodney!

And suddenly, discordantly, a thought slipped and flashed sideways across the panorama of Joan's mind, much as she had noticed a snake flash and slip across the dust coloured track in front of the car only yesterday – a mere streak of writhing green, gone almost before you saw it.

The streak consisted of three words, leaping out of space and back into oblivion.

The Randolph girl . . .

Gone again before she had time to note them consciously.

Blanche was cheerfully contrite.

'Sorry, Joan. Let's come into the other room and have coffee. I always did have a vulgar mind, you know.'

'Oh no,' the protest came quickly to Joan's lips, genuine and slightly shocked.

Blanche looked amused.

'Oh yes, don't you remember? Remember the time I slipped out to meet the baker's boy?'

Joan winced. She had forgotten that incident. At the time it had seemed daring and – yes – actually romantic. Really a vulgar and unpleasant episode.

Blanche, settling herself in a wicker chair and calling to the boy to bring coffee, laughed to herself.

'Horrid precocious little piece I must have been. Oh, well, that's always been my undoing. I've always been far too fond of men. And always rotters! Extraordinary, isn't it? First Harry – and *he* was a bad lot all right – though frightfully good looking. And then Tom who never amounted to much, though I was fond of him in a way. Johnnie Pelham – that was a good time while it lasted. Gerald wasn't much good, either . . .'

At this point the boy brought the coffee, thus interrupting what Joan could not but feel was a singularly unsavoury catalogue.

Blanche caught sight of her expression.

'Sorry, Joan, I've shocked you. Always a bit strait-laced, weren't you?'

'Oh, I hope I'm always ready to take a broad-minded view.'

Joan achieved a kindly smile.

She added rather awkwardly:

'I only mean I'm – I'm so *sorry*.'

'For me?' Blanche seemed amused by the idea. 'Nice of you, darling, but don't waste sympathy. I've had lots of fun.'

Joan could not resist a swift sideways glance. Really, had Blanche any idea of the deplorable appearance she presented? Her carelessly dyed hennaed hair, her somewhat dirty, flamboyant clothes, her haggard, lined face, an old woman – an old raddled woman – an old disreputable gipsy of a woman!

Blanche, her face suddenly growing grave, said soberly:

'Yes, you're quite right, Joan. You've made a success of your life. And I – well, I've made a mess of mine. I've gone down in the world and you've gone – no, you've stayed where you were – a St Anne's girl who's married suitably and always been a credit to the old school!'

Trying to steer the conversation towards the only ground that she and Blanche had in common now, Joan said:

'Those were good days, weren't they?'

'So-so.' Blanche was careless in her praise. 'I got bored sometimes. It was all so smug and consciously healthy. I wanted to get out and see the world. Well,' her mouth gave a humorous twist, 'I've seen it. I'll say I've seen it!'

For the first time Joan approached the subject of Blanche's presence in the rest house.

'Are you going back to England? Are you leaving on the convoy tomorrow morning?'

Her heart sank just a little as she put the question. Really, she did not want Blanche as a travelling companion. A chance meeting was all very well, but she had grave doubts of being able to sustain the pose of friendship all the way across Europe. Reminiscences of the old days would soon wear thin.

Blanche grinned at her.

'No, I'm going the other way. To Baghdad. To join my husband.'

'Your husband?'

Joan really felt quite surprised that Blanche should have anything so respectable as a husband.

'Yes, he's an engineer – on the railway. Donovan his name is.'

'Donovan?' Joan shook her head. 'I don't think I came across him at all.'

Blanche laughed.

'You wouldn't, darling. Rather out of your class. He drinks like a fish anyway. But he's got a heart like a child. And it may surprise you, but he thinks the world of me.'

'So he ought,' said Joan loyally and politely.

'Good old Joan. Always play the game, don't you? You must be thankful I'm not going the other way. It would break even your Christian spirit to have five days of my company. You needn't trouble to deny it. I know what I've become. Coarse in mind and body – that's what you were thinking. Well, there are worse things.'

Joan privately doubted very much whether there were. It seemed to her that Blanche's decadence was a tragedy of the first water.

Blanche went on:

'Hope you have a good journey, but I rather doubt it. Looks to me as though the rains are starting. If so, you may be stuck for days, miles from anywhere.'

'I hope not. It will upset all my train reservations.'

'Oh well, desert travel is seldom according to schedule. So long as you get across the wadis all right, the rest will be easy. And of course the drivers take plenty of food and water along. Still it gets a bit boring to be stuck somewhere with nothing to do but think.'

Joan smiled.

'It might be rather a pleasant change. You know, one never has time as a rule to relax at all. I've often wished I could have just one week with really nothing to do.'

'I should have thought you could have had that whenever you liked?'

'Oh no, my dear. I'm a very busy woman in my small way. I'm the Secretary of the Country Gardens Association – And I'm on the committee of our local hospital. And there's the Institute – and the Guides. And I take quite an active part in politics. What with all that and running the house and then Rodney and I go out a good deal and have people in to see us. It's so good for a lawyer to have plenty of social background, I always think. And then I'm very fond of my garden and like to do quite a good deal in it myself. Do you know, Blanche, that there's hardly a moment, except perhaps a quarter of an hour before dinner, when I can really sit down and rest? And to keep up with one's reading is quite a task.'

'You seem to stand up to it all pretty well,' murmured Blanche, her eyes on the other's unlined face.

'Well, to wear out is better than to rust out! And I must admit I've always had marvellous health. I really *am* thankful for that. But all the same it would be wonderful to feel that one had a whole day or even two days with nothing to do but think.'

'I wonder,' said Blanche, 'what you'd think about?'

Joan laughed. It was a pleasant, tinkling, little sound.

'There are always plenty of things to think about, aren't there?' she said.

Blanche grinned.

'One can always think of one's sins!'

'Yes, indeed.' Joan assented politely though without amusement.

Blanche eyed her keenly.

'Only that wouldn't give *you* occupation long!'

She frowned and went on abruptly:

'You'd have to go on from them to think of your good deeds. And all the blessings of your life! Hm – I don't know. Might be rather dull. I wonder,' she paused, 'if you'd nothing to think about but yourself for days and days I wonder what you'd find out about yourself –'

Joan looked sceptical and faintly amused.

'Would one find out anything one didn't know before?'

Blanche said slowly:

'I think one might . . .' She gave a sudden shiver. 'I shouldn't like to try it.'

'Of course,' said Joan, 'some people have an urge towards the contemplative life. I've never been able to understand that myself. The mystic point of view is very difficult to appreciate. I'm afraid I haven't got that kind of religious temperament. It always seems to me to be rather extreme, if you know what I mean.'

'It's certainly simpler,' said Blanche, 'to make use of the shortest prayer that is known.' And in answer to

Joan's inquiring glance she said abruptly, '"God be merciful to me, a sinner." That covers pretty well everything.'

Joan felt slightly embarrassed.

'Yes,' she said. 'Yes, it certainly does.'

Blanche burst out laughing.

'The trouble with you, Joan, is that you're *not* a sinner. That cuts you off from prayer! Now I'm well equipped. It seems to me sometimes that I've never ceased doing the things that I ought not to have done.'

Joan was silent because she didn't know quite what to say.

Blanche resumed again in a lighter tone:

'Oh well, that's the way of the world. You quit when you ought to stick, and you take on a thing that you'd better leave alone; one minute life's so lovely you can hardly believe it's true – and immediately after that you're going through a hell of misery and suffering! When things are going well you think they'll last for ever – and they never do – and when you're down under you think you'll never come up and breathe again. That's what life is, isn't it?'

It was so entirely alien to any conception Joan had of life or to life as she had known it that she was unable to make what she felt would be an adequate response.

With a brusque movement Blanche rose to her feet.

'You're half asleep, Joan. So am I. And we've got an early start. It's been nice seeing you.'

The two women stood a minute, their hands clasped. Blanche said quickly and awkwardly, with a sudden, rough tenderness in her voice:

'Don't worry about your Barbara. She'll be all right – I'm sure of it. Bill Wray is a good sort, you know – and there's the kid and everything. It was just that she was very young and the kind of life out here – well, it goes to a girl's head sometimes.'

Joan was conscious of nothing but complete bewilderment.

She said sharply:

'I don't know what you mean.'

Blanche merely looked at her admiringly.

'That's the good old school tie spirit! Never admit anything. You really haven't changed a bit, Joan. By the way I owe you twenty-five pounds. Never thought of it until this minute.'

'Oh, don't bother about that.'

'No fear.' Blanche laughed. 'I suppose I meant to pay it back, but after all if one ever does lend money to people one knows quite well one will never see one's money again. So I haven't worried much. You were a good sport, Joan – that money was a godsend.'

'One of the children had to have an operation, didn't he?'

'So they thought. But it turned out not to be necessary after all. So we spent the money on a bender and got a roll-top desk for Tom as well. He'd had his eye on it for a long time.'

Moved by a sudden memory, Joan asked:

'Did he ever write his book on Warren Hastings?'

Blanche beamed at her.

'Fancy your remembering that! Yes, indeed, a hundred and twenty thousand words.'

'Was it published?'

'Of course not! After that Tom started on a life of Benjamin Franklin. That was even worse. Funny taste, wasn't it? I mean such dull people. If I wrote a life, it would be of someone like Cleopatra, some sexy piece – or Casanova, say, something spicy. Still, we can't all have the same ideas. Tom got a job again in an office – not so good as the other. I'm always glad, though, that he had his fun. It's awfully important, don't you think, for people to do what they really want to do?'

'It rather depends,' said Joan, 'on circumstances. One has to take so many things into consideration.'

'Haven't you done what you wanted to do?'

'I?' Joan was taken aback.

'Yes, *you*,' said Blanche. 'You wanted to marry Rodney Scudamore, didn't you? And you wanted children? And a comfortable home.' She laughed and added, 'And to live happily ever afterwards, world without end, Amen.'

Joan laughed too, relieved at the lighter tone the conversation had taken.

'Don't be ridiculous. I've been very lucky, I know.'

And then, afraid that that last remark had been tactless when confronted by the ruin and bad luck that had been Blanche's lot in life, she added hurriedly:

'I really *must* go up now. Good night – and it's been marvellous seeing you again.'

She squeezed Blanche's hand warmly (would Blanche expect her to kiss her? Surely not.) and ran lightly up the stairs to her bedroom.

Poor Blanche, thought Joan as she undressed, neatly laying and folding her clothes, putting out a fresh pair of stockings for the morning. Poor Blanche. It's really too tragic.

She slipped into her pyjamas and started to brush her hair.

Poor Blanche. Looking so awful and so coarse.

She was ready for bed now, but paused irresolutely before getting in.

One didn't, of course, say one's prayers every night. In fact it was quite a long time since Joan had said a prayer of any kind. And she didn't even go to church very often.

But one did, of course, *believe*.

And she had a sudden odd desire to kneel down now by the side of this rather uncomfortable looking bed (such nasty cotton sheets, thank goodness she had got her own soft pillow with her) and well – say them properly – like a child.

The thought made her feel rather shy and uncomfortable.

She got quickly into bed and pulled up the covers. She picked up the book that she had laid on the little table by the bed head, *The Memoirs of Lady Catherine Dysart* – really most entertainingly written – a very witty account of mid-Victorian times.

She read a line or two but found she could not concentrate.

I'm too tired, she thought.

She laid down the book and switched off the light.

Again the thought of prayer came to her. What was it that Blanche had said so outrageously – 'that cuts you off from prayer.' Really, what did she mean?

Joan formed a prayer quickly in her mind – a prayer of isolated words strung together.

God – thank thee – poor Blanche – thank thee that *I* am not like that – great mercies – all my blessings – and especially not like poor Blanche – poor Blanche – really dreadful. Her own fault of course – dreadful – quite a shock – thank God – I am different – poor Blanche . . .

Joan fell asleep.

Chapter Two

It was raining when Joan Scudamore left the rest house the following morning, a fine gentle rain that seemed somehow incongruous in this part of the world.

She found that she was the only passenger going west – a sufficiently uncommon occurrence, it appeared, although there was not much traffic this time of year. There had been a large convoy on the preceding Friday.

A battered looking touring car was waiting with a European driver and a native relief driver. The manager of the rest house was on the steps in the grey dawn of the morning to hand Joan in, yell at the Arabs until they adjusted the baggage to his satisfaction, and to wish Mademoiselle, as he called all his lady guests, a safe and comfortable journey. He bowed magnificently and handed her a small cardboard container in which was her lunch.

The driver yelled out cheerily:

'Bye bye, Satan, see you tomorrow night or next week – and it looks more like next week.'

The car started off. It wound through the streets of the oriental city with its grotesque and unexpected blocks of occidental architecture. The horn blared, donkeys swerved aside, children ran. They drove out through the western gate and on to a broad, unequally paved road that looked important enough to run to the world's end.

Actually it petered out abruptly after two kilometres and an irregular track took its place.

In good weather it was, Joan knew, about seven hours' run to Tell Abu Hamid which was the present terminus of the Turkish railway. The train from Stamboul arrived there this morning and would go back again at eight-thirty this evening. There was a small rest house at Tell Abu Hamid for the convenience of travellers, where they were served with what meals they might need. They should meet the convoy coming east about half-way along the track.

The going was now very uneven. The car leapt and jumped and Joan was thrown up and down in her seat.

The driver called back that he hoped she was all right. It was a bumpy bit of track but he wanted to hurry as much as possible in case he had difficulty crossing the two wadis they had to negotiate.

From time to time he looked anxiously up at the sky.

The rain began to fall faster and the car began to do a series of skids, zigzagging to and fro and making Joan feel slightly sick.

They reached the first wadi about eleven. There was water in it, but they got across and after a slight peril of sticking on the hill up the other side drew out of it successfully. About two kilometres farther on they ran into soft ground and stuck there.

Joan slipped on her mackintosh coat and got out, opening her box of lunch and eating as she walked up and down and watched the two men working, digging with spades, flinging jacks at each other, putting boards they had brought with them under the wheels. They swore and toiled and the wheels spun angrily in the air. It seemed to Joan an impossible task, but the driver assured her that it wasn't a bad place at all. Finally, with unnerving suddenness the wheels bit and roared, and the car quivered forward on to drier ground.

A little farther on they encountered two cars coming in the opposite direction. All three stopped and the drivers held a consultation, giving each other recommendations and advice.

In the other cars were a woman and a baby, a young French officer, an elderly Armenian and two commercial looking Englishmen.

Presently they went on. They stuck twice more and again the long, laborious business of jacking up and digging out had to be undertaken. The second wadi was more difficult of negotiation than the first one. It was dusk when they came to it and the water was rushing through it.

Joan asked anxiously:

'Will the train wait?'

'They usually give an hour's grace. They can make up that on the run, but they won't delay beyond nine-thirty. However the track gets better from now on. Different kind of ground – more open desert.'

They had a bad time clearing the wadi – the farther bank was sheer slippery mud. It was dark when the car at last reached dry ground. From then on, the going was better but when they got to Tell Abu Hamid it was a quarter past ten and the train to Stamboul had gone.

Joan was so completely done up that she hardly noticed her surroundings.

She stumbled into the rest house dining-room with its trestle tables, refused food but asked for tea and then went straight to the dimly lit, bleak room with its three iron beds and taking out bare necessaries, she tumbled into bed and slept like a log.

She awoke the next morning her usual cool competent self. She sat up in bed and looked at her watch. It was half past nine. She got up, dressed and came out into the dining-room. An Indian with an artistic turban wrapped round his head appeared and she ordered breakfast. Then she strolled to the door and looked out.

With a slight humorous grimace she acknowledged to herself that she had indeed arrived at the middle of nowhere.

This time, she reflected, it looked like taking about double the time.

On her journey out she had flown from Cairo to Baghdad. This route was new to her. It was actually seven days from Baghdad to London – three days in the train from London to Stamboul, two days on to Aleppo, another night to the end of the railway at Tell Abu Hamid, then a day's motoring, a night in a rest house and another motor drive to Kirkuk and on by train to Baghdad.

There was no sign of rain this morning. The sky was blue and cloudless, and all around was even coloured golden brown sandy dust. From the rest house itself a tangle of barbed wire enclosed a refuse dump of tins and a space where some skinny chickens ran about squawking loudly. Clouds of flies had settled on such tins as had recently contained nourishment. Something that looked like a bundle of dirty rags suddenly got up and proved to be an Arab boy.

A little distance away, across another tangle of barbed wire was a squat building that was evidently the station with something that Joan took to be either an artesian well or a big water tank beside it. On the far horizon to the north was the faint outline of a range of hills.

Apart from that, nothing. No landmarks, no buildings, no vegetation, no human kind.

A station, a railway track, some hens, what seemed to be a disproportionate amount of barbed wire – and that was all.

Really, Joan thought, it was very amusing. Such an odd place to be held up.

The Indian servant came out and said that the Memsahib's breakfast was ready.

Joan turned and went in. The characteristic atmosphere of a rest house, gloom, mutton fat, paraffin and Flit greeted her with a sense of rather distasteful familiarity.

There was coffee and milk (tinned milk), a whole dish

of fried eggs, some hard little rounds of toast, a dish of jam, and some rather doubtful looking stewed prunes.

Joan ate with a good appetite. And presently the Indian reappeared and asked what time the Memsahib would like lunch.

Joan said not for a long time – and it was agreed that half past one would be a satisfactory hour.

The trains, as she knew, went three days a week, on Monday, Wednesday and Friday. It was Tuesday morning, so she would not be able to leave until tomorrow night. She spoke to the man asking if that was correct.

'That right, Memsahib. Miss train last night. Very unfortunate. Track very bad, rain very heavy in night. That means no cars can go to and fro from here to Mosul for some days.'

'But the trains will be all right?'

Joan was not interested in the Mosul track.

'Oh yes, train come all right tomorrow morning. Go back tomorrow night.'

Joan nodded. She asked about the car which had brought her.

'Go off this morning early. Driver hope get through. But I think not. I think him stick one, two days on way there.'

Again without much interest Joan thought it highly probable.

The man went on giving information.

'That station, Memsahib, over there.'

Joan said that she had thought, somehow, that it might be the station.

'Turkish station. Station in Turkey. Railway Turkish. Other side of wire, see. That wire frontier.'

Joan looked respectfully at the frontier and thought what very odd things frontiers were.

The Indian said happily:

'Lunch one-thirty exactly,' and went back into the rest

house. A minute or two later she heard him screaming in a high angry voice from somewhere at the back of it. Two other voices chimed in. A spate of high, excited Arabic filled the air.

Joan wondered why it was always Indians who seemed to be in charge of rest houses like this one. Perhaps they had had experience of European ways. Oh well, it didn't much matter.

What should she do with herself this morning? She might go on with the amusing *Memoirs of Lady Catherine Dysart*. Or she might write some letters. She could post them when the train got to Aleppo. She had a writing pad and some envelopes with her. She hesitated on the threshold of the rest house. It was so dark inside and it smelt so. Perhaps she would go for a walk.

She fetched her thick double felt hat – not that the sun was really dangerous at this time of year, still it was better to be careful. She put on her dark glasses and slipped the writing pad and her fountain pen into her bag.

Then she set out, past the refuse dump and the tins, in the opposite direction to the railway station, since there might, possibly, be international complications if she tried to cross the frontier.

She thought to herself, How curious it is walking like this . . . there's nowhere to walk *to*.

It was a novel and rather interesting idea. Walking on the downs, on moorland, on a beach, down a road – there was always some objective in view. Over that hill, to that clump of trees, to that patch of heather, down this lane to the farm, along the high road to the next town, by the side of the waves to the next cove.

But here it was *from* – not to. Away from the rest house – that was all. Right hand, left hand, straight ahead – just bare dun-coloured horizon.

She strolled along not too briskly. The air was pleasant. It was hot, but not too hot. A thermometer, she thought, would have registered seventy. And there was a faint, a very faint breeze.

She walked for about ten minutes before turning her head.

The rest house and its sordid accompaniments had receded in a very accommodating manner. From here it looked quite pleasant. Beyond it, the station looked like a little cairn of stones.

Joan smiled and strolled on. Really the air was delicious! There was a purity in it, a freshness. No staleness here, no taint of humanity or civilization. Sun and sky and sandy earth, that was all. Something a little intoxicating in its quality. Joan took deep breaths into her lungs. She was enjoying herself. Really this was quite an adventure! A most welcome break in the monotony of existence. She was quite glad she had missed the train. Twenty-four hours of absolute quiet and peace would be good for her. It was not as though there were any absolute urgency in her return. She could wire to Rodney from Stamboul explaining the delay.

Dear old Rodney! She wondered what he was doing now. Not, really, that there was anything to wonder about, because she knew. He would be sitting in his office at Alderman, Scudamore and Witney's – quite a nice room on the first floor looking out over the Market Square. He had moved into it when old Mr Witney died. He liked that room – She remembered how she had come in one day to see him and had found him standing by the window staring out at the market (it was market day) and at a herd of cattle that was being driven in. 'Nice lot of shorthorns – those,' he had said. (Or perhaps it wasn't shorthorns – Joan wasn't very good at farming terms – but something like that, anyway.) And she had said, 'About the new boiler for the central heating, I think Galbraith's estimate is far too high. Shall I see what Chamberlain would charge?'

She remembered the slow way Rodney had turned, taking off his glasses and rubbing his eyes and looking at her in an absent faraway manner as though he didn't really see her, and the way he had said '*boiler*?' as though it was some difficult and remote subject he had never heard of, and then saying – really rather stupidly, 'I believe Hoddesdon's selling that young bull of his. Wants the money, I suppose.'

She thought it was very nice of Rodney to be so interested in old Hoddesdon at Lower Mead farm. Poor old man, everyone knew he was going down the hill. But she did wish Rodney would be a little quicker at listening to what was said to him. Because, after all, people expected a lawyer to be sharp and alert, and if Rodney was to look at clients in that vague way it might create quite a bad impression.

So she had said with quick, affectionate impatience:

'Don't *wool-gather*, Rodney. It's the *boiler* I'm talking about for the *central heating*.' And Rodney had said certainly have a second estimate but that costs were bound to be higher and they must just make up their minds to it. And then he had glanced at the papers piled up on his desk and she had said that she mustn't keep him – it looked as though he had a lot of work to do.

Rodney smiled and said that as a matter of fact he had got a lot of work piled up – and he'd been wasting time already watching the market. 'That's why I like this room,' he said. 'I look forward to Fridays. Listen to 'em now.'

And he had held up his hand, and she had listened and heard a good deal of mooing and lowing – really a very confused and rather ugly noise of cattle and sheep – but Rodney, funnily enough, seemed to like it. He stood there, his head a little on one side, smiling . . .

Oh well, it would not be market day today. Rodney would be at his desk with no distractions. And her fears about clients thinking Rodney vague had been quite unfounded. He was by far the most popular member of the firm. Everyone liked him which was half the battle in a country solicitor's practice.

And but for me, thought Joan proudly, he'd have turned the whole thing down!

Her thoughts went to that day when Rodney had told her about his uncle's offer.

It was an old-fashioned flourishing family business and it had always been understood that Rodney should go into it after he had passed his law exams. But Uncle Harry's offer of a partnership and on such excellent terms was an unexpectedly happy occurrence.

Joan had expressed her own delight and surprise and had congratulated Rodney warmly before she noticed that Rodney didn't seem to be sharing in her sentiments. He had actually uttered the incredible words, 'If I accept –'

She had exclaimed dismayed, 'But Rodney!'

Clearly she remembered the white set face he had turned to her. She hadn't realized before what a nervous person Rodney was. His hands picking up blades of turf were trembling. There was a curious pleading look in his dark eyes. He said:

'I hate office life. I hate it.'

Joan was quick to sympathize.

'Oh I know, darling. It's been awfully stuffy and hard work and just sheer grind – not even interesting. But a partnership is different – I mean you'll have an interest in the whole thing.'

'In contracts, leases, messuages, covenants, whereas, insomuch as heretofore –'

Some absurd legal rigmarole he had trotted out, his mouth laughing, his eyes sad and pleading – pleading so hard with her. And she loved Rodney so much!

'But it's always been understood that you'd go into the firm.'

'Oh I know, I know. But how was I to guess I'd hate it so?'

'But – I mean – what else – what do you want to do?'

And he had said, very quickly and eagerly, the words pouring out in a rush:

'I want to farm. There's Little Mead coming into the market. It's in a bad state – Horley's neglected it – but that's why one could get it cheap – and it's good land, mark you . . .'

And he had hurried on, outlining plans, talking in such technical terms that she had felt quite bewildered for she herself knew nothing of wheat or barley or the rotation of crops, or of pedigreed stocks or dairy herds.

She could only say in a dismayed voice:

'Little Mead – but that's right out under Asheldown – *miles* from anywhere.'

'It's good land, Joan – and a good position . . .'

He was off again. She'd had no idea that Rodney could be so enthusiastic, could talk so much and with such eagerness.

She said doubtfully, 'But darling, would you ever make a living out of it?'

'A living? Oh yes – a bare living anyway.'

'That's what I mean. People always say there's no money in farming.'

'Oh, there isn't. Not unless you're damned lucky – or unless you've got a lot of capital.'

'Well, you see – I mean, it isn't *practical.*'

'Oh, but it is, Joan. I've got a little money of my own, remember, and with the farm paying its way and making a bit over we'd be all right. And think of the wonderful life we'd have! It's grand, living on a farm!'

'I don't believe you know anything about it.'

'Oh yes, I do. Didn't you know my mother's father was a big farmer in Devonshire? We spent our holidays there as children. I've never enjoyed myself so much.'

It's true what they say, she had thought, men are just like children . . .

She said gently, 'I daresay – but life isn't holidays. We've got the future to think of, Rodney. There's Tony.'

For Tony had been a baby of eleven months then.

She added, 'And there may be – others.'

He looked a quick question at her, and she smiled and nodded.

'But don't you see, Joan, that makes it all the better? It's a good place for children, a farm. It's a healthy place. They have fresh eggs and milk, and run wild and learn how to look after animals.'

'Oh but, Rodney, there are lots of other things to consider. There's their schooling. They must go to good schools. And that's expensive. And boots and clothes and teeth and doctors. And making nice friends for them. You can't just do what *you* want to do. You've got to consider children if you bring them into the world. After all, you've got a duty to them.'

Rodney said obstinately, but there was a question in his voice this time, 'They'd be happy . . .'

'It's not practical, Rodney, really it isn't. Why, if you go into the firm you may be making as much as two thousand pounds a year some day.'

'Easily, I should think. Uncle Harry makes more than that.'

'There! You see! You can't turn a thing like that down. It would be madness!'

She had spoken very decidedly, very positively. She had got, she saw, to be firm about this. She must be wise for the two of them. If Rodney was blind to what was best for him, she must assume the responsibility. It was so dear and silly and ridiculous, this farming idea. He was like a little boy. She felt strong and confident and maternal.

'Don't think I don't understand and sympathize,

Rodney,' she said. 'I do. But it's just one of those things that isn't real.'

He had interrupted to say that farming was real enough.

'Yes, but it's just not in the picture. *Our* picture. Here you've got a wonderful family business with a first class opening in it for you – and a really quite amazingly generous proposition from your uncle – '

'Oh, I know. It's far better than I ever expected.'

'And you can't – you simply *can't* turn it down! You'd regret it all your life if you did. You'd feel horribly guilty.'

He muttered, 'That bloody office!'

'Oh, Rodney, you don't really hate it as much as you think you do.'

'Yes, I do. I've been in it five years, remember. I ought to know what I feel.'

'You'll get used to it. And it will be different now. Quite different. Being a partner, I mean. And you'll end by getting quite interested in the work – and in the people you come across. You'll see, Rodney – you'll end by being perfectly happy.'

He had looked at her then – a long sad look. There had been love in it, and despair and something else, something that had been, perhaps, a last faint flicker of hope . . .

'How do you know,' he had asked, 'that I shall be happy?'

And she had answered briskly and gaily, 'I'm quite sure you will. You'll see.'

And she had nodded brightly and with authority.

He had sighed and said abruptly: 'All right then. Have it your own way.'

Yes, Joan thought, that was really a very narrow shave. How lucky for Rodney that she had held firm and not allowed him to throw away his career for a mere passing craze! Men, she thought, would make sad messes of their lives if it weren't for women. Women had stability, a sense of reality . . .

Yes, it was lucky for Rodney he'd had her.

She glanced down at her wrist watch. Half past ten. No point in walking too far – especially (she smiled) as there was nowhere to walk to.

She looked over her shoulder. Extraordinary, the rest house was nearly out of sight. It had settled down into the landscape so that you hardly saw it. She thought, I must be careful not to walk too far. I might get lost.

A ridiculous idea – no – perhaps not so ridiculous after all. Those hills in the distance, you could hardly see them now – they were indistinguishable from cloud. The station didn't exist.

Joan looked round her with appreciation. Nothing. No one.

She dropped gracefully to the ground. Opening her bag she took out her writing pad and her fountain pen. She'd write a few letters. It would be amusing to pass on her sensations.

Who should she write to? Lionel West? Janet Annesmore? Dorothea? On the whole, perhaps, Janet.

She unscrewed the cap of her fountain pen. In her easy flowing handwriting she began to write:

> Dearest Janet: You'll never guess where I'm writing this letter! In the middle of the desert. I'm marooned here between trains – they only go three times a week.
>
> There's a rest house with an Indian in charge of it and a lot of hens and some peculiar looking Arabs and me. There's no one to talk to and nothing to do. I can't tell you how I am enjoying it.
>
> The desert air is wonderful – so incredibly fresh. And the stillness, you'd have to feel it to understand. It's as though for the first time for years I could hear

myself think! One leads such a dreadfully busy life, always rushing from one thing to the other. It can't be helped, I suppose, but one ought really to make time for intervals of thought and recuperation.

I've only been here half a day but I feel miles better already. No people. I never realized how much I wanted to get away from people. It's soothing to the nerves to know that all round you for hundreds of miles there's nothing but sand and sun . . .

Joan's pen flowed on, evenly, over the paper.

Chapter Three

Joan stopped writing and glanced at her watch.

A quarter past twelve.

She had written three letters and her pen had now run out of ink. She noted, too, that she had nearly finished her writing pad. Rather annoying, that. There were several more people she could have written to.

Although, she mused, there was a certain sameness in writing after a while . . . The sun and the sand and how lovely it was to have time to rest and think! All quite true – but one got tired of trying to phrase the same facts slightly differently each time . . .

She yawned. The sun had really made her feel quite sleepy. After lunch she would lie on her bed and have a sleep.

She got up and strolled slowly back towards the rest house.

She wondered what Blanche was doing now. She must have reached Baghdad – she had joined her husband. The husband sounded rather a dreadful kind of man. Poor Blanche – dreadful to come down in the world like that. If it hadn't been for that very good-looking young vet, Harry Marston – if Blanche had met some nice man like Rodney. Blanche herself had said how charming Rodney was.

Yes, and Blanche had said something else. What was it? Something about Rodney's having a roving eye. Such a common expression – and quite untrue! *Quite* untrue! Rodney had never – never once –

The same thought as before, but not so snakelike in its rapidity, passed across the surface of Joan's mind.

The Randolph girl . . .

Really, thought Joan indignantly, walking suddenly just a little faster as though to outpace some unwelcome thought, I can't imagine why I keep thinking of the Randolph girl. It's not as though Rodney . . .

I mean, there's nothing in it . . .

Nothing at all . . .

It was simply that Myrna Randolph was that kind of a girl. A big, dark, luscious looking girl. A girl who, if she took a fancy to a man, didn't seem to have any reticence about advertising the fact.

To speak plainly, she'd made a dead set at Rodney. Kept saying how wonderful he was. Always wanted him for a partner at tennis. Had even got a habit of sitting at parties devouring him with her eyes.

Naturally Rodney had been a little flattered. Any man would have been. In fact, it would have been quite ridiculous if Rodney hadn't been flattered and pleased by the attentions of a girl years younger than he was and one of the best looking girls in the town.

Joan thought to herself, if I hadn't been clever and tactful about the whole thing . . .

She reviewed her conduct with a gentle glow of self-approbation. She had handled the situation very well – very well indeed. The light touch.

'Your girl friend's waiting for you, Rodney. Don't keep her waiting . . . Myrna Randolph of course . . . Oh yes, she is, darling . . . Really she makes herself quite ridiculous sometimes.'

Rodney had grumbled.

'I don't want to play tennis with the girl. Put her in that other set.'

'Now don't be ungracious, Rodney. You must play with her.'

That was the right way to handle things – lightly – playfully. Showing quite well that she knew that there couldn't be anything serious in it . . .

It must have been rather nice for Rodney – for all that he growled and pretended to be annoyed. Myrna Randolph was the kind of girl that practically every man found attractive. She was capricious and treated her admirers with deep contempt, saying rude things to them and then beckoning them back to her with a sideways glance of the eyes.

Really, thought Joan (with a heat that was unusual in her) a most detestable girl. Doing everything she could to break up my married life.

No, she didn't blame Rodney. She blamed the girl. Men were so easily flattered. And Rodney had been married then about – what – ten years? Eleven? Ten years was what writers called a dangerous period in married life. A time when one or the other party had a tendency to run off the rails. A time to get through warily until you settled down beyond it into comfortable, set ways.

As she and Rodney had . . .

No she didn't blame Rodney – not even for that kiss she had surprised.

Under the mistletoe indeed!

That was what the girl had had the impudence to say when she came into the study.

'We're christening the mistletoe, Mrs Scudamore. Hope you don't mind.'

Well, Joan thought, I kept my head and didn't show anything.

'Now, hands off my husband, Myrna! Go and find some young man of your own.'

And she had laughingly chivvied Myrna out of the room. Taking it all as a joke.

And then Rodney had said, 'Sorry, Joan. But she's an attractive wench – and it's Christmas time.'

He had stood there smiling at her, apologizing, but not looking really sheepish or upset. It showed that the thing hadn't really gone far.

And it shouldn't go any farther! She had made up her mind to that. She had taken every care to keep Rodney out of Myrna Randolph's way. And the following Easter Myrna had got engaged to the Arlington boy.

So really the whole incident amounted to exactly nothing at all. Perhaps there had been just a little fun in it for Rodney. Poor old Rodney – he really deserved a little fun. He worked so hard.

Ten years – yes, it was a dangerous time. Even she herself, she remembered, had felt a certain restlessness . . .

That rather wild looking young man, that artist – what was his name now? Really she couldn't remember. Hadn't she been a little taken with him herself?

She admitted to herself with a smile that she really had been – yes – just a little silly about him. He had been so earnest – had stared at her with such disarming intensity. Then he had asked if she would sit for him.

An excuse, of course. He had done one or two charcoal sketches and then torn them up. He couldn't 'get' her on canvas, he had said.

Joan remembered her own subtly flattered, pleased feelings. Poor boy, she had thought, I'm afraid he really is getting rather fond of me . . .

Yes, that had been a pleasant month . . .

Though the end of it had been rather disconcerting. Not at all according to plan. In fact, it just showed that Michael Callaway (Callaway, that was his name, of course!) was a thoroughly unsatisfactory sort of person.

They had gone for a walk together, she remembered, in Haling Woods, along the path where the Medaway comes twisting down from the summit of Asheldown. He had asked her to come in a rather gruff, shy voice.

She had envisaged their probable conversation. He

would tell her, perhaps, that he loved her, and she would be very sweet and gentle and understanding and a little – just a little – regretful. She thought of several charming things she might say, things that Michael might like to remember afterwards.

But it hadn't turned out like that.

It hadn't turned out like that at all!

Instead, Michael Callaway had, without warning, seized her and kissed her with a violence and a brutality that had momentarily deprived her of breath, and letting go of her had observed in a loud and self-congratulatory voice:

'My God, I wanted that!' and had proceeded to fill a pipe, with complete unconcern and apparently deaf to her angry reproaches.

He had merely said, stretching his arms and yawning, 'I feel a lot better now.'

It was exactly, thought Joan, remembering the scene, what a man might say after downing a glass of beer on a thirsty day.

They had walked home in silence after that – in silence on Joan's part, that is. Michael Callaway seemed, from the extraordinary noises he made, to be attempting to sing. It was on the outskirts of the wood, just before they emerged on to the Crayminster Market Wopling high road, that he had paused and surveyed her dispassionately, and then remarked in a contemplative tone:

'You know, you're the sort of woman who ought to be raped. It might do you good.'

And, whilst she had stood, speechless with anger and astonishment, he had added cheerfully:

'I'd rather like to rape you myself – and see if you looked the least bit different afterwards.'

Then he had stepped out on to the high road, and giving up trying to sing had whistled cheerfully.

Naturally she had never spoken to him again and he had left Crayminster a few days later.

A strange, puzzling and rather disturbing incident. Not an incident that Joan had cared to remember. In fact, she rather wondered that she had remembered it now . . .

Horrid, the whole thing had been, quite horrid.

She would put it out of her mind at once. After all, one didn't want to remember unpleasant things when one was having a sun and sand rest cure. There was so much to think of that was pleasant and stimulating.

Perhaps lunch would be ready. She glanced at her watch, but saw that it was only a quarter to one.

When she got back to the rest house, she went to her room and hunted in her suitcase to see if she had any more writing paper with her. No, she hadn't. Oh, well, it didn't matter really. She was tired of writing letters. There wasn't much to say. You couldn't go on writing the same thing. What books had she got? *Lady Catherine*, of course. And a detective story that William had given her last thing. Kind of him, but she didn't really care for detective stories. And *The Power House* by Buchan. Surely that was a very old book. She had read it years ago.

Oh well, she would be able to buy some more books at the station at Aleppo.

Lunch consisted of an omelette (rather tough and overcooked), curried eggs, and a dish of salmon (tinned) and baked beans and tinned peaches.

It was rather a heavy meal. After it Joan went and lay down on her bed. She slept for three quarters of an hour, then woke up and read *Lady Catherine Dysart* until tea time.

She had tea (tinned milk) and biscuits and went for a stroll and came back and finished *Lady Catherine Dysart*. Then she had dinner: omelette, curried salmon and rice, a dish of eggs and baked beans and tinned apricots. After that she started the detective story and finished it by the time she was ready for bed.

The Indian said cheerfully:

'Good night, Memsahib. Train come in seven-thirty tomorrow morning but not go out till evening, half past eight.'

Joan nodded.

There would be another day to put in. She'd got *The Power House* still. A pity it was so short. Then an idea struck her.

'There will be travellers coming in on the train? Oh, but they go straight off to Mosul, I suppose?'

The man shook his head.

'Not tomorrow, I think. No cars arrive today. I think track to Mosul very bad. Everything stick for many days.'

Joan brightened. There would be travellers off the train in the rest house tomorrow. That would be rather nice – there was sure to be someone to whom it would be possible to talk.

She went to bed feeling more cheerful than she had ten minutes ago. She thought. There's something about the atmosphere of this place – I think it's that dreadful smell of rancid fat! It quite depresses one.

She awoke the next morning at eight o'clock and got up and dressed. She came out into the dining-room. One place only was laid at the table. She called, and the Indian came in.

He was looking excited.

'Train not come, Memsahib.'

'Not come? You mean it's late?'

'Not come at all. Very heavy rain down line – other side Nissibin. Line all wash away – no train get through for three four five six days perhaps.'

Joan looked at him in dismay.

'But then – what do I do?'

'You stay here, Memsahib. Plenty food, plenty beer, plenty tea. Very nice. You wait till train come.'

Oh dear, thought Joan, these Orientals. Time means nothing to them.

She said, 'Couldn't I get a car?'

He seemed amused.

'Motor car? Where would you get motor car? Track to Mosul very bad, everything stuck other side of wadi.'

'Can't you telephone down the line?'

'Telephone where? Turkish line. Turks very difficult people – not do anything. They just run train.'

Joan thought, rallying with what she hoped was amusement, This really *is* being cut off from civilization! No telephones or telegraphs, no cars.

The Indian said comfortingly:

'Very nice weather, plenty food, all very comfortable.'

Well, Joan thought, it's certainly nice weather. That's lucky. Awful if I had to sit inside this place all day.

As though reading her thoughts, the man said:

'Weather good here, very seldom rain. Rain nearer Mosul, rain down the line.'

Joan sat down at the laid place at the table and waited for her breakfast to be brought. She had got over her momentary dismay. No good making a fuss – she had much too much sense for that. These things couldn't be helped. But it was rather an annoying waste of time.

She thought with a half smile: It looks as though what I said to Blanche was a wish that has come true. I said I should be glad of an interval to rest my nerves. Well, I've got it! Nothing whatever to do here. Not even anything to read. Really it ought to do me a lot of good. Rest cure in the desert.

The thought of Blanche brought some slightly unpleasant association – something that, quite definitely, she didn't want to remember. In fact, why think of Blanche at all?

She went out after breakfast. As before, she walked a reasonable distance from the rest house and then sat down on the ground. For some time she sat quite still, her eyes half closed.

Wonderful, she thought, to feel this peace and quiet oozing into her. She could simply *feel* the good it was doing her. The healing air, the lovely warm sun – the peace of it all.

She remained so for a little longer. Then she glanced at her watch. It was ten minutes past ten.

She thought: The morning is passing quite quickly . . .

Supposing she were to write a line to Barbara? Really it was extraordinary that she hadn't thought of writing to Barbara yesterday instead of those silly letters to friends in England.

She got out the pad and her pen.

> 'Darling Barbara,' she wrote. 'I'm not having a very lucky journey. Missed Monday night's train and now I'm held up here for days apparently. It's very peaceful and lovely sunshine so I'm quite happy.'

She paused. What to say next. Something about the baby – or William? What on earth could Blanche have meant – '*don't worry about Barbara*'. Of course! That was why Joan hadn't wanted to think about Blanche. Blanche had been so peculiar in the things she had said about Barbara.

As though she, Barbara's mother, wouldn't know anything there was to know about her own child.

'*I'm sure she'll be all right now.*' Did that mean that things *hadn't* been all right?

But in what way? Blanche had hinted that Barbara was too young to have married.

Joan stirred uneasily. At the time, she remembered, Rodney had said something, of the kind. He had said, quite suddenly, and in an unusually peremptory way:

'I'm not happy about this marriage, Joan.'

'Oh, Rodney, but *why*? He's so nice and they seem so well suited.'

'He's a nice enough young fellow – but she doesn't love him, Joan.'

She'd been astonished – absolutely astonished.

'Rodney – really – how *ridiculous*! Of *course* she's in love with him! Why on earth would she want to marry him otherwise?'

He had answered – rather obscurely: 'That's what I'm afraid of.'

'But, darling – *really* – aren't you being a little ridiculous?'

He had said, paying no attention to her purposely light tone, 'If she doesn't love him, she mustn't marry him. She's too young for that – and she's got too much temperament.'

'Well, really, Rodney, what do *you* know about temperament?'

She couldn't help being amused.

But Rodney didn't even smile. He said, 'Girls do marry sometimes – just to get away from home.'

At that she had laughed outright.

'Not homes like Barbara's! Why, no girl ever had a happier home life.'

'Do you really think that's true, Joan?'

'Why, of course. Everything's always been perfect for the children here.'

He said slowly, 'They don't seem to bring their friends to the house much.'

'Why, darling, I'm always giving parties and asking young people! I make a point of it. It's Barbara herself who's always saying she doesn't want parties and not to ask people.'

Rodney had shaken his head in a puzzled, unsatisfied way.

And later, that evening, she had come into the room just as Barbara was crying out impatiently:

'It's no good, Daddy, I've got to get away. I can't stand it any longer – and don't tell me to go and take a job somewhere, because I should hate that.'

'What's all this?' Joan said.

After a pause, a very slight pause, Barbara had explained, a mutinous flush on her check.

'Just Daddy thinking he knows best! He wants me to be engaged for years. I've told him I can't stand that and I want to marry William and go away to Baghdad. I think it will be wonderful out there.'

'Oh dear,' said Joan anxiously. 'I wish it wasn't so far away. I'd like to have you under my eye as it were.'

'Oh, *Mother*!'

'I know, darling, but you don't realize how young you are, how inexperienced. I should be able to help you so much if you were living somewhere not too far away.'

Barbara had smiled and had said, 'Well, it looks as though I shall have to paddle my own canoe without the benefit of your experience and wisdom.'

And as Rodney was going slowly out of the room, she had rushed after him and had suddenly flung her arms round his neck hugging him and saying, 'Darling Dads. Darling, darling, darling . . .'

Really, thought Joan, the child is becoming quite demonstrative. But it showed, at any rate, how entirely wrong Rodney was in his ideas. Barbara was just revelling in the thought of going out East with her William – and very nice it was to see two young things in love and so full of plans for the future.

Extraordinary that an idea should have got about Baghdad that Barbara had been unhappy at home. But it was a place that seemed absolutely full of gossip and rumours, so much so that one hardly liked to mention anyone.

Major Reid, for instance.

She herself had never met Major Reid, but he had been mentioned quite often in Barbara's letters home. Major Reid had been to dinner. They were going shooting with Major Reid. Barbara was going for the summer months up to Arkandous. She and another young married woman had shared a bungalow and Major Reid had been up there at the same time. They had had a lot of tennis. Later, Barbara and he had won the mixed doubles at the club.

So it had really been quite natural for Joan to ask brightly about Major Reid – she had heard so much about him, she said, that she was really longing to see him.

It was quite ludicrous the embarrassment her question had caused. Barbara had turned quite white, and William had gone red, and after a minute or two he had grunted out in a very odd voice:

'We don't see anything of him now.'

His manner had been so forbidding that she really hadn't liked to say anything more. But afterwards when Barbara had gone to bed Joan reopened the subject, saying smilingly, that she seemed to have put her foot in it. She'd had an idea that Major Reid was quite an intimate friend.

William got up and tapped his pipe against the fireplace.

'Oh, I dunno,' he said vaguely. 'We did a bit of shooting together and all that. But we haven't seen anything of him for a long time now.'

It wasn't, Joan thought, very well done. She had smiled to herself, men were so transparent. She was a little amused at William's old-fashioned reticence. He probably thought of her as a very prim, strait-laced woman – a regular mother-in-law.

'I see,' she said. 'Some scandal.'

'What do you mean?' William had turned on her quite angrily.

'My dear boy!' Joan smiled at him. 'It's quite obvious from your manner. I suppose you found out something about him and had to drop him. Oh, I shan't ask questions. These things are very painful, I know.'

William said slowly, 'Yes – yes, you're right. They *are* painful.'

'One takes people so much at their own valuation,' said Joan. 'And then, when one finds out that one has been mistaken in them, it's all so awkward and unpleasant.'

'He's cleared out of this country, that's one good thing,' said William. 'Gone to East Africa.'

And suddenly Joan remembered some scraps of conversation overheard one day at the Alwyah Club. Something about Nobby Reid going to Uganda.

A woman had said, 'Poor Nobby, it's really not his fault that every little idiot in the place runs after him.'

And another, older, woman had laughed spitefully and said, 'He takes a lot of trouble with them. Dewy innocents – that's what Nobby likes. The unsophisticated bride. And I must say he has a wonderful technique! He can be terribly attractive. The girl always thinks he's passionately in love with her. That's usually the moment when he's just thinking of passing on to the next one.'

'Well,' said the first woman. '*We* shall all miss him. He's so amusing.'

The other laughed.

'There's a husband or two who won't be sorry to see him go! As a matter of fact very few men like him.'

'He's certainly made this place too hot to hold him.'

Then the second woman had said, 'Hush,' and lowered her voice and Joan hadn't heard any more. She had hardly noticed the conversation at the time, but it came back to her now, and she felt curious.

If William didn't want to talk about it, perhaps Barbara might be less reticent.

But instead of that Barbara had said quite clearly and rather disagreeably:

'I don't want to talk about him, Mother, do you mind?'

Barbara, Joan reflected, never did want to talk about anything. She had been quite incredibly reticent and touchy about her illness, and its cause. Some form of poisoning had started it all, and naturally Joan had taken it to be food poisoning of some kind. Ptomaine poisoning was very common in hot climates, so she believed. But both William and Barbara had been most unwilling to go into details – and even the doctor to whom she had naturally applied for information as Barbara's mother, had been taciturn and uncommunicative. His principal care was to stress the point that young Mrs Wray must not be questioned or encouraged to dwell on her illness.

'All she needs now is care and building up. Whys and wherefores are very unprofitable subjects of discussion and talking about all that will do the patient no good. That's just a hint I'm giving you, Mrs Scudamore.'

An unpleasant, dour kind of man, Joan had found him, and not at all impressed, as he easily might have been, by the devotion of a mother in rushing out from England post haste.

Oh well, Barbara had been grateful, at all events. At least Joan supposed so . . . She had certainly thanked her mother very prettily. William, too, had said how good of her it was.

She had said how she wished she could have stayed on, and William had said, Yes, he wished so too. And she had said now they mustn't press her – because it was really too tempting and she'd love to have a winter in Baghdad – but after all there was Barbara's father to consider, and it wouldn't be fair on him.

And Barbara, in a faint little voice had said, 'Darling Dads,' and after a moment or two had said, 'Look here, Mother, why don't you stay?'

'You must think of your father, darling.'

Barbara said in that rather curious dry voice she used sometimes that she *was* thinking of him, but Joan said, no, she couldn't leave poor dear Rodney to servants.

There was a moment, a few days before her departure, when she had almost changed her mind. She might, at any rate, stay another month. But William had pointed out so eloquently the uncertainties of desert travel if she left it too late in the season that she had been quite alarmed and had decided that it was best to stick to her original plan. After that William and Barbara had been so nice to her that she almost changed her mind again – but not quite.

Though really, however late in the season she had left it, nothing could be much worse than this.

Joan looked at her watch again. Five minutes to eleven. One seemed to be able to think a great deal in quite a short space of time.

She rather wished she'd brought *The Power House* out here with her, though perhaps as it was the only thing she had to read it was wise to keep it back – something in reserve.

Two hours to put in before lunch time. She had said she would have lunch at one o'clock today. Perhaps she had better walk on a little, only it seemed rather silly just walking aimlessly with nowhere particular to walk to. And the sun was quite hot.

Oh well, how often she had wished she could have just a little time to herself, to think things out. Now, if ever, was her opportunity. What things were there that she had wanted to think out so urgently?

Joan searched her mind – but they seemed mostly to have been matters of local importance – remembering where she had put this, that or the other, deciding how to arrange the servants' summer holidays, planning the redecorating of the old schoolroom.

All these things seemed now rather remote and unimportant. November was rather far in advance to plan the servants' holidays, and besides, she had to know when Whitsuntide was and that needed next year's almanac. She could, however, decide about the schoolroom. The walls a light shade of beige and oatmeal covers with some nice bright cushions? Yes, that would do very well.

Ten minutes past eleven. Redecorating and doing up the schoolroom hadn't taken long!

Joan thought vaguely, If I'd only known, I could have brought along some interesting book on modern science and discoveries, something that would explain things like the quantum theory.

And then she wondered what had put the quantum theory into her head and thought to herself, Of course – the covers – and Mrs Sherston.

For she remembered that she had once been discussing the vexed questions of chintzes or cretonnes for drawing-room covers with Mrs Sherston, the bank manager's wife – and right in the middle of it Mrs Sherston had said in her abrupt way, 'I do wish I was clever enough to understand the quantum theory. It's such a fascinating idea, isn't it, energy all done up in little parcels.'

Joan had stared at her, for she really couldn't see what scientific theories had to do with chintzes, and Mrs Sherston had got rather red and said, 'Stupid of me, but you know the way things come into your head quite suddenly – and it *is* an exciting idea, isn't it?'

Joan hadn't thought the idea particularly exciting and the conversation had ended there. But she remembered quite well Mrs Sherston's own cretonne – or rather hand-printed linen covers. A design of leaves in browns and greys and reds. She had said, 'These are very unusual, were they very expensive?' And Mrs Sherston had said yes, they were. And she had added that she had got them because she loved woods and trees and the dream of her life was to go somewhere like Burma or Malaya where things grew really *fast*! Really fast, she had added, in an anxious tone, and making a rather clumsy gesture with her hands to express impatience.

Those linens, reflected Joan now, must have cost at least eighteen and six a yard, a fantastic price for those days. One ought, by realizing what Captain Sherston gave his wife for housekeeping and furnishing, to have had at least an inkling of what was to come out later.

She herself had never really liked the man. She remembered sitting in his office at the bank, discussing the reinvestment of some shares, Sherston opposite her, behind his desk – a great big breezy man exuding *bonhomie*. A rather exaggeratedly social manner . . . 'I'm a man of the world, dear lady,' he seemed to be saying, 'don't think of me as just a money machine – I'm a tennis player, a golfer, a dancer, a bridge player. The real me is the chap you meet at a party, not the official who says "no further overdraft".'

A great overblown windbag, thought Joan indignantly. Crooked, always crooked. Even then he must have started on his falsification of the books, or whatever the swindle was. And yet nearly everyone had liked him, had said what a good sort old Sherston was, not at all the usual type of bank manager.

Well, that was true enough. The usual type of bank manager doesn't embezzle bank funds.

Well, Leslie Sherston had, at any rate, got her hand-printed linen covers out of it all. Not that anyone had ever suggested that an extravagant wife had led to Sherston's dishonesty. You only had to look at Leslie Sherston to see that money meant nothing particularly to her. Always wearing shabby green tweeds and grubbing around in her garden or tramping through the countryside. She never bothered much about the children's clothes, either. And once, much later, Joan remembered an afternoon when

Leslie Sherston had given her tea, fetching a big loaf and a roll of butter and some homemade jam and kitchen cups and teapots – everything bundled anyhow on a tray and brought in. An untidy, cheerful, careless sort of woman, with a one-sided slouch when she walked and a face that seemed all on one side too, but that one-sided smile of hers was rather nice, and people liked her on the whole.

Ah, well, poor Mrs Sherston. She'd had a sad life, a very sad life.

Joan moved restlessly. Why had she let that phrase, a sad life, come into her mind? It reminded her of Blanche Haggard (though that was quite a different kind of sad life!) and thinking of Blanche brought her back again to Barbara and the circumstances surrounding Barbara's illness. Was there nothing one could think of that did not lead in some painful and undesired direction?

She looked at her watch once more. At any rate, hand-printed linens and poor Mrs Sherston had taken up nearly half an hour. What could she think about now? Something pleasant, with no disturbing sidelines.

Rodney was probably the safest subject to think about. Dear Rodney. Joan's mind dwelt pleasurably on the thought of her husband, visualizing him as she had last seen him on the platform at Victoria, saying goodbye to her just before the train pulled out.

Yes, dear Rodney. Standing there looking up at her, the sun shining full on his face and revealing so mercilessly the network of little lines at the corners of his eyes – such tired eyes. Yes, tired eyes, eyes full of a deep sadness. (Not, she thought, that Rodney *is* sad. It's just a trick of construction. Some animals have sad eyes.) Usually, too, he was wearing his glasses and then you didn't notice the sadness of his eyes. But he certainly looked a very tired man. No wonder, when he worked so hard. He practically never took a day off. (I shall change all that when I get back, thought Joan. He must have more leisure. I ought to have thought of it before.)

Yes, seen there in the bright light, he looked as old or older than his years. She had looked down on him and he up at her and they had exchanged the usual idiotic last words.

'I don't think you have to go through any Customs at Calais.'

'No, I believe one goes straight through to the Simplon express.'

'Brindisi carriage, remember. I hope the Mediterranean behaves.'

'I wish I could stop off a day or two in Cairo.'

'Why don't you?'

'Darling, I must hurry to Barbara. It's only a weekly air service.'

'Of course. I forgot.'

A whistle blew. He smiled up at her.

'Take care of yourself, little Joan.'

'Goodbye, don't miss me too much.'

The train started with a jerk. Joan drew her head in. Rodney waved, then turned away. On an impulse she leaned out again. He was already striding up the platform.

She felt a sudden thrill at seeing that well-known back. How young he looked suddenly, his head thrown back, his shoulders squared. It gave her quite a shock . . .

She had an impression of a young, carefree man striding up the platform.

It reminded her of the day she had first met Rodney Scudamore.

She had been introduced to him at a tennis party and they had gone straight on to the court.

He had said: 'Shall I play at the net?'

And it was then that she had looked after him as he strode up to take his place at the net and thought what a very attractive back he had . . . the easy confident way he walked, the set of his head and neck . . .

Suddenly she had been nervous. She had served two lots of double faults running and had felt all hot and bothered.

And then Rodney had turned his head and smiled at her encouragingly – that kind, friendly smile of his. And she had thought what a very attractive young man . . . and she had proceeded straight away to fall in love with him.

Looking out from the train, watching Rodney's retreating back until the sight of it was blotted out by the people on the platform, she relived that summer's day so many years ago.

It was as though the years had fallen away from Rodney, leaving him once more an eager, confident young man.

As though the years had fallen away . . .

Suddenly, in the desert, with the sun pouring down on her, Joan gave a quick uncontrollable shiver.

She thought, No, no – I don't want to go on – I don't want to think about this . . .

Rodney, striding up the platform, his head thrown back, the tired sag of his shoulders all gone. A man who had been relieved of an intolerable burden . . .

Really, what was the matter with her? She was imagining things, inventing them. Her eyes had played a trick on her.

Why hadn't he waited to see the train pull out?

Well, why should he? He was in a hurry to get through what business he had to do in London. Some people didn't like to see trains go out of stations bearing away someone they loved.

Really it was impossible that anyone could remember so clearly as she did exactly how Rodney's back had looked!

She was imagining –

Stop, that didn't make it any better. If you imagined a thing like that, it meant that such an idea was already in your head.

And it couldn't be true – the inference that she had drawn simply could not be true.

She was saying to herself (wasn't she?) that Rodney was glad she was going away . . .

And that simply couldn't be true!

Chapter Four

Joan arrived back at the rest house definitely overheated. Unconsciously she had increased her pace so as to get away from that last unwelcome thought.

The Indian looked at her curiously and said:

'Memsahib walk very fast. Why walk fast? Plenty time here.'

Oh God, thought Joan, plenty time indeed!

The Indian and the rest house and the chickens and the tins and the barbed wire were all definitely getting on her nerves.

She went on into her bedroom and found *The Power House.*

At any rate, she thought, it's cool in here and dark.

She opened *The Power House* and began to read.

By lunch time she had read half of it.

There was omelette for lunch and baked beans round it, and after it there was a dish of hot salmon with rice, and tinned apricots.

Joan did not eat very much.

Afterwards she went to her bedroom and lay down.

If she had a touch of the sun from walking too fast in the heat, a sleep would do her good.

She closed her eyes but sleep did not come.

She felt particularly wide awake and intelligent.

She got up and took three aspirins and lay down again.

Every time she shut her eyes she saw Rodney's back going away from her up the platform. It was insupportable!

She pulled aside the curtain to let in some light and got

The Power House. A few pages before the end she dropped asleep.

She dreamt that she was going to play in a tournament with Rodney. They had difficulty in finding the balls but at last they got to the court. When she started to serve she found that she was playing against Rodney and the Randolph girl. She served nothing but double faults. She thought, Rodney will help me, but when she looked for him she could not find him. Everyone had left and it was getting dark. I'm all alone, thought Joan. I'm all alone.

She woke up with a start.

'I'm all alone,' she said aloud.

The influence of the dream was still upon her. It seemed to her that the words she had just said were terribly frightening.

She said again, 'I'm all alone.'

The Indian put his head in.

'Memsahib call?'

'Yes,' she said. 'Get me some tea.'

'Memsahib want tea? Only three o'clock.'

'Never mind, I want tea.'

She heard him going away and calling out, 'Chai-chai!'

She got up from the bed and went over to the fly-spotted mirror. It was reassuring to see her own normal, pleasant looking face.

'I wonder,' said Joan addressing her reflection, 'whether you can be going to be ill? You're behaving very oddly.'

Perhaps she *had* got a touch of the sun?

When the tea came she was feeling quite normal again. In fact the whole business was really very funny. She, Joan Scudamore, indulging in *nerves*! But of course it wasn't nerves, it was a touch of the sun. She wouldn't go out again until the sun was well down.

She ate some biscuits and drank two cups of tea. Then she finished *The Power House.* As she closed the book, she was assailed by a definite qualm.

She thought, Now I've got nothing to read.

Nothing to read, no writing materials, no sewing with her. Nothing at all to do, but wait for a problematical train that mightn't come for days.

When the Indian came in to clear tea away she said to him:

'What do you do here?'

He seemed surprised by the question.

'I look after travellers, Memsahib.'

'I know.' She controlled her impatience. 'But that doesn't take you all your time?'

'I give them breakfast, lunch, tea.'

'No, no, I don't mean that. You have helpers?'

'Arab boy – very stupid, very lazy, very dirty – I see to everything myself, not trust boy. He bring bath water – throw away bath water – he help cook.'

'There are three of you, then, you, the cook, the boy? You must have a lot of time when you aren't working. Do you read?'

'Read? Read what?'

'Books.'

'I not read.'

'Then what do you do when you're not working?'

'I wait till time do more work.'

It's no good, thought Joan. You can't talk to them. They don't know what you mean. This man, he's here always, month after month. Sometimes, I suppose, he gets a holiday, and goes to a town and gets drunk and sees friends. But for weeks on end he's here. Of course he's got the cook and the boy . . . The boy lies in the sun and sleeps when he isn't working. Life's as simple as that for him. They're no good to me, not any of them. All the English this man knows is eating and drinking and 'Nice weather.'

The Indian went out. Joan strolled restlessly about the room.

'I mustn't be foolish. I must make some kind of plan. Arrange a course of – of thinking for myself. I really must *not* allow myself to get – well – rattled.'

The truth was, she reflected, that she had always led such a full and occupied life. So much interest in it. It was a civilized life. And if you had all that balance and proportion in your life, it certainly left you rather at a loss when you were faced with the barren uselessness of doing nothing at all. The more useful and cultured a woman you were, the more difficult it made it.

There were some people, of course, even at home, who often sat about for hours doing nothing. Presumably they would take to this kind of life quite happily.

Even Mrs Sherston, though as a rule she was active and energetic enough for two, had occasionally sat about doing nothing. Usually when she was out for walks. She would walk with terrific energy and then drop down suddenly on a log of wood, or a patch of heather and just sit there staring into space.

Like that day when she, Joan, had thought it was the Randolph girl . . .

She blushed slightly as she remembered her own actions.

It had, really, been rather like spying. The sort of thing that made her just a little ashamed. Because she wasn't, really, that kind of woman.

Still, with a girl like Myrna Randolph . . .

A girl who didn't seem to have any moral sense . . .

Joan tried to remember how it had all come about.

She had been taking some flowers to old Mrs Garnett and had just come out of the cottage door when she had heard Rodney's voice in the road outside the hedge. His voice and a woman's voice answering him.

She had said goodbye to Mrs Garnett quickly and come out into the road. She was just able to catch sight of Rodney and, she felt sure, the Randolph girl, swinging round the corner of the track that led up to Asheldown.

No, she wasn't very proud of what she had done then. But she had felt, at the time, that she had to know. It wasn't exactly Rodney's fault – everyone knew what Myrna Randolph was.

Joan had taken the path that went up through Haling Wood and had come out that way on to the bare shoulder of Asheldown and at once she had caught sight of them – two figures sitting there motionless staring down over the pale, shining countryside below.

The relief when she had seen that it wasn't Myrna Randolph at all, but Mrs Sherston! They weren't even sitting close together. There were four feet at least between them. Really, a quite ridiculous distance – hardly friendly! But then Leslie Sherston wasn't really a very friendly person – not, that is, a demonstrative one. And she certainly could not be regarded as a siren – the mere idea would have been ludicrous. No, she had been out on one of her tramps and Rodney had overtaken her and with his usual friendly courtesy, had accompanied her.

Now, having climbed up Asheldown Ridge, they were resting for a while and enjoying the view before going back again.

Astonishing, really, the way that neither of them moved nor spoke. Not, she thought, very companionable. Oh well, presumably they both had their own thoughts. They felt, perhaps, that they knew each other well enough not to have to bother to talk or to make conversation.

For by that time, the Scudamores had got to know Leslie Sherston very much better. The bombshell of Sherston's defalcations had burst upon a dismayed Crayminster and Sherston himself was by now serving his prison sentence. Rodney was the solicitor who had acted for him at the trial and who also acted for Leslie. He had been very sorry for Leslie, left with two small children and no money. Everybody had been prepared to be sorry for poor Mrs Sherston and if they had not gone on being quite so sorry that was entirely Leslie Sherston's own fault. Her resolute cheerfulness had rather shocked some people.

'She must, I think,' Joan had said to Rodney, 'be rather insensitive.'

He had replied brusquely that Leslie Sherston had more courage than anyone he had ever come across.

Joan had said, 'Oh, yes, *courage*. But courage isn't everything!'

'Isn't it?' Rodney had said. He'd said it rather queerly. Then he'd gone off to the office.

Courage was a virtue one would certainly not deny to Leslie Sherston. Faced with the problem of supporting herself and two children, and with no particular qualifications for the task she had managed it.

She'd gone to work at a market gardener's until she was thoroughly conversant with the trade, accepting in the meantime a small allowance from an aunt, and living with the children in rooms. Thus, when Sherston had come out of prison, he'd found her established in a different part of the world altogether, growing fruit and vegetables for the market. He'd driven the truck in and out from the nearby town, and the children had helped and they'd managed somehow to make not too bad a thing of it. There was no doubt that Mrs Sherston had worked like a Trojan and it was particularly meritorious because she must, at that time, have begun to suffer a good deal of pain from the illness that eventually killed her.

Oh well, thought Joan, presumably she loved the man. Sherston had certainly been considered a good-looking man and a favourite with women. He looked rather different when he came out of prison. She, Joan, had only seen him once, but she was shocked by the change in him. Shifty-eyed, deflated, still boastful, still attempting to bluff and bluster. A wreck of a man. Still, his wife had loved him and stuck by him and for that Joan respected Leslie Sherston.

She had, on the other hand, considered that Leslie had been absolutely wrong about the children.

That same aunt who had come to the rescue financially when Sherston was convicted had made a further offer when he was due to come out of prison.

She would, she said, adopt the younger boy, and an uncle, persuaded by her, would pay the school fees of the elder boy and she herself would take them both for the holidays. They could take the uncle's name by deed poll and she and the uncle would make themselves financially responsible for their future.

Leslie Sherston had turned this offer down unconditionally and in that Joan thought she had been selfish. She was refusing for her children a much better life than she could give them and one free from any taint of disgrace.

However much she loved her boys, she ought, Joan thought, and Rodney agreed with her, to think of their lives before her own.

But Leslie had been quite unyielding and Rodney had washed his hands of the whole matter. He supposed, he had said with a sigh, that Mrs Sherston knew her own business best. Certainly, Joan thought, she was an obstinate creature.

Walking restlessly up and down the rest house floor, Joan remembered Leslie Sherston as she had looked that day sitting on Asheldown Ridge.

Sitting hunched forward, her elbows on her knees, her chin supported on her hands. Sitting curiously still. Looking out across the farmland and the plough to where slopes of oaks and beeches in Little Havering wood were turning golden red.

She and Rodney sitting there – so quiet – so motionless – staring in front of them.

Quite why she did not speak to them, or join them, Joan hardly knew.

Perhaps it was the guilty consciousness of her suspicions of Myrna Randolph?

Anyhow she had not spoken to them. Instead she had gone quietly back into the shelter of the trees and had taken her way home. It was an incident that she had never liked very much to think about – and she had certainly never mentioned it to Rodney. He might think she had ideas in her head, ideas about him and Myrna Randolph.

Rodney walking up the platform at Victoria . . .

Oh goodness, surely she wasn't going to begin *that* all over again?

What on earth had put that extraordinary notion into her head? That Rodney (who was and always had been devoted to her) was enjoying the prospect of her absence?

As though you could tell anything by the way a man walked!

She would simply put the whole ridiculous fancy out of her mind.

She wouldn't think any more about Rodney, not if it made her imagine such curious and unpleasant things.

Up to now, she'd never been a fanciful woman.

It *must* be the sun.

Chapter Five

The afternoon and evening passed with interminable slowness.

Joan didn't like to go out in the sun again until it was quite low in the sky. So she sat in the rest house.

After about half an hour she felt it unendurable to sit still in a chair. She went into the bedroom and began to unpack her cases and repack them. Her things, so she told herself, were not properly folded. She might as well make a good job of it.

She finished the job neatly and expeditiously. It was five o'clock. She might safely go out now surely. It was so depressing in the rest house. If only she had something to read . . .

Or even, thought Joan desperately, a wire puzzle!

Outside she looked with distaste at the tins and the hens and the barbed wire. What a horrible place this was. Utterly horrible.

She walked, for a change, in a direction parallel with the railway line and the Turkish frontier. It gave her a feeling of agreeable novelty. But after a quarter of an hour the effect was the same. The railway line, running a quarter of a mile to her right, gave her no feeling of companionship.

Nothing but silence – silence and sunlight.

It occurred to Joan that she might recite poetry. She had always been supposed as a girl to recite and read poetry very well. Interesting to see what she could remember after all these years. There was a time when she had known quite a lot of poetry by heart.

The quality of mercy is not strained,
It droppeth as the gentle rain from heaven

What came next? Stupid. She simply couldn't remember.

Fear no more the heat of the sun

(That began comfortingly anyway! Now how did it go on?)

Nor the furious winter's rages
Thou thy worldly task has done
Home art gone and ta'en thy wages
Golden lads and girls all must
As chimney sweepers come to dust.

No, not very cheerful on the whole. Could she remember any of the sonnets? She used to know them. The *marriage of true minds* and that one that Rodney had asked her about.

Funny the way he had said suddenly one evening:

'*And thy eternal summer shall not fade* – that's from Shakespeare, isn't it?'

'Yes, from the sonnets.'

And he had said:

'*Let me not unto the marriage of true minds admit impediment*? That one?'

'No, the one that begins, *Shall I compare thee to a summer's day.*'

And then she had quoted the whole sonnet to him, really rather beautifully, with a lot of expression and all the proper emphasis.

At the end, instead of expressing approbation, he had only repeated thoughtfully:

'*Rough winds do shake the darling buds of May*... but it's October now, isn't it?'

It was such an extraordinary thing to say that she had stared at him. Then he had said:

'Do you know the other one? The one about the marriage of true minds?'

'Yes.' She paused a minute and then began:

'Let me not to the marriage of true minds
Admit impediments. Love is not love
Which alters where it alteration finds,
Or bends with the remover to remove:
O, no, it is an ever-fixed mark
That looks on tempests and is never shaken,
It is the star to every wandering bark
Whose worth's unknown, although his height be taken.
Love's not Time's fool, though rosy lips and cheeks
Within his bending sickle's compass come;
Love alters not with his brief hours and weeks,
But bears it out even to the edge of doom.
If this be error, and upon me prov'd
I never writ, nor no man ever lov'd.'

She finished, giving the last lines full emphasis and dramatic fervour.

'Don't you think I recite Shakespeare rather well? I was always supposed to at school. They said I read poetry with a lot of expression.'

But Rodney had only answered absently, 'It doesn't really need expression. Just the words will do.'

She had sighed and murmured, 'Shakespeare *is* wonderful, isn't he?'

And Rodney had answered, 'What's really so wonderful is that he was just a poor devil like the rest of us.'

'Rodney, what an extraordinary thing to say.'

He had smiled at her, then, as though waking up. 'Is it?'

Getting up, he had strolled out of the room murmuring as he went:

'Rough winds do shake the darling buds of May
And summer's lease hath all too short a date.'

Why on earth, she wondered, had he said, 'But it's October now'?

What could he have been thinking about?

She remembered that October, a particularly fine and mild one.

Curious, now she came to think of it, the evening that Rodney had asked her about the sonnets had been the actual evening of the day when she had seen him sitting with Mrs Sherston on Asheldown. Perhaps Mrs Sherston had been quoting Shakespeare, but it wasn't very likely. Leslie Sherston was not, she thought, at all an intellectual woman.

It had been a wonderful October that year.

She remembered quite plainly, a few days later, Rodney asking her in a bewildered tone:

'Ought this thing to be out this time of year?'

He was pointing to a rhododendron. One of the early flowering ones that normally bloom in March or the end of February. It had a rich blood red blossom and the buds were bursting all over it.

'No,' she had told him. 'Spring is the time, but sometimes they do come out in autumn if it's unusually mild and warm.'

He had touched one of the buds gently with his fingers and had murmured under his breath:

'The darling buds of May.'

March, she told him, not May.

'It's like blood,' he said, 'heart's blood.'

How unlike Rodney, she thought, to be so interested in flowers.

But after that he had always liked that particular rhododendron.

She remembered how, many years later, he had worn a great bud of it in his buttonhole.

Much too heavy, of course, and it had fallen out as she knew it would.

They'd been in the churchyard, of all extraordinary places, at the time.

She'd seen him there as she came back past the church and had joined him and said, 'Whatever are you doing here, Rodney?'

He had laughed and said, 'Considering my latter end, and what I'll have put on my tombstone. Not granite chips, I think, they're so genteel. And certainly not a stout marble angel.'

They had looked down then at a very new marble slab which bore Leslie Sherston's name.

Following her glance Rodney had spelled out slowly:

'Leslie Adeline Sherston, dearly beloved wife of Charles Edward Sherston, who entered into rest on 11th May, 1930. And God shall wipe away their tears.'

Then, after a moment's pause, he had said:

'Seems damned silly to think of Leslie Sherston under a cold slab of marble like that, and only a congenital idiot like Sherston would ever have chosen that text. I don't believe Leslie ever cried in her life.'

Joan had said, feeling just a little shocked and rather as though she was playing a slightly blasphemous game:

'What would you choose?'

'For her? I don't know. Isn't there something in the Psalms? *In thy presence is the fullness of joy*. Something like that.'

'I really meant for yourself.'

'Oh, for me?' He thought for a minute or two – smiled to himself. '*The Lord is my shepherd. He leadeth me in green pastures*. That will do very well for me.'

'It sounds rather a dull idea of Heaven, I've always thought.'

'What's your idea of Heaven, Joan?'

'Well – not all the golden gates and that stuff, of course. I like to think of it as a *state*. Where everyone is busy helping, in some wonderful way, to make this world, perhaps, more beautiful and happier. Service – that's my idea of Heaven.'

'What a dreadful little prig you are, Joan.' He had laughed in his teasing way to rob the words of their sting. Then he had said, 'No, a green valley – that's good enough for me – and the sheep following the shepherd home in the cool of the evening –'

He paused a minute and then said, 'It's an absurd fancy of mine, Joan, but I play with the idea sometimes that, as I'm on my way to the office and go along the High Street, I turn to take the alley into the Bell Walk and instead of the alley I've turned into a hidden valley, with green pasture and soft wooded hills on either side. It's been there all the time, existing secretly in the heart of the town. You turn from the busy High Street into it and you feel quite bewildered and say perhaps, "Where am I?" And then they'd tell you, you know, very gently, that you were dead . . .'

'Rodney!' She was really startled, dismayed. 'You – you're ill. You can't be well.'

It had been her first inkling of the state he was in – the precursor of that nervous breakdown that was shortly to send him for some two months to the sanatorium in Cornwall where he seemed content to lie silently listening to the gulls and staring out over the pale, treeless hills to the sea.

But she hadn't realized until that day in the churchyard that he really had been overworking. It was as they turned to go home, she with an arm through his, urging him forward, that she saw the heavy rhododendron bud drop from his coat and fall on Leslie's grave.

'Oh, look,' she said, 'your rhododendron,' and she stooped to pick it up. But he had said quickly:

'Let it lie. Leave it there for Leslie Sherston. After all – she was our friend.'

And Joan had said quickly, what a nice idea, and that

she would bring a big bunch of those yellow chrysanthemums herself tomorrow.

She had been, she remembered, a little frightened by the queer smile he gave her.

Yes, definitely she had felt that there was something wrong with Rodney that evening. She didn't, of course, realize that he was on the edge of a complete breakdown, but she did know that he was, somehow, different . . .

She had plied him with anxious questions all the way home but he hadn't said much. Only repeated again and again:

'I'm tired, Joan . . . I'm very tired.'

And once, incomprehensibly, 'We can't *all* be brave . . .'

It was only about a week later that he had, one morning, said dreamily, 'I shan't get up today.'

And he had lain there in bed, not speaking or looking at anyone, just lain there, smiling quietly.

And then there had been doctors and nurses and finally the arrangements for him to go for a long rest cure to Trevelyan. No letters or telegrams and no visitors. They wouldn't even let Joan come and see him. Not his own wife.

It had been a sad, perplexing, bewildering time. And the children had been very difficult too. Not helpful. Behaving as though it was all her, Joan's, fault.

'Letting him slave and slave and slave at that office. You know perfectly well, Mother, Father's worked far too hard for years.'

'I know, my dears. But what could I do about it?'

'You ought to have yanked him out of it years ago. Don't you *know* he hates it? Don't you know *anything* about Father?'

'That's quite enough, Tony. Of course I know all about your father – far more than you do.'

'Well, sometimes I don't think so. Sometimes I don't think you know anything about *anybody*.'

'Tony – really!'

'Dry up, Tony –' That was Averil. 'What's the good?'

Averil was always like that. Dry, unemotional, affecting a cynicism and a detached outlook beyond her years. Averil, Joan sometimes thought despairingly, had really no heart at all. She disliked caresses and was always completely unaffected by appeals to her better self.

'Darling Daddy –' It was a wail from Barbara, younger than the other two, more uncontrolled in her emotions. 'It's all your fault, Mother. You've been cruel to him – *cruel* – always.'

'Barbara!' Joan quite lost patience. 'What do you think you're talking about? If there is one person who comes first in this house, it's your father. How do you think you could all have been educated and clothed and fed if your father hadn't worked for you? He's sacrificed himself for *you* – that's what parents have to do – and they do it without making any fuss about it.'

'Let me take this opportunity of thanking you, Mother,' said Averil, 'for all the sacrifices *you* have made for us.'

Joan looked at her daughter doubtfully. She suspected Averil's sincerity. But surely the child couldn't be so impertinent . . .

Tony distracted her attention. He was asking gravely:

'It's true, isn't it, that Father once wanted to be a farmer?'

'A farmer? No, of course he didn't. Oh well, I believe years ago – just a kind of boyish fancy. But the family have always been lawyers. It's a family firm, and really quite famous in this part of England. You ought to be very proud of it, and glad that you're going into it.'

'But I'm not going into it, Mother. I want to go to East Africa and farm.'

'Nonsense, Tony. Don't let's have this silly nonsense all over again. Of course you're going into the firm! You're the only son.'

'I'm not going to be a lawyer, Mother. Father knows and he's promised me.'

She stared at him, taken aback, shaken by his cool certainty.

Then she sank into a chair, tears came to her eyes. So unkind, all of them, browbeating her like this.

'I don't know what's come over you all – talking to me like this. If your father were here – I think you are all behaving very unkindly!'

Tony had muttered something and, turning, had slouched out of the room.

Averil, in her dry voice, said, 'Tony's quite set on being a farmer, Mother. He wants to go to an agricultural college. It seems quite batty to me. I'd much rather be a lawyer if I was a man. I think the law is jolly interesting.'

'I never thought,' sobbed Joan, 'that my children could be so unkind to me.'

Averil had sighed deeply. Barbara, still sobbing hysterically in a corner of the room, had called out:

'I know Daddy will die. I know he will – and then we'll be all alone in the world. I can't bear it. Oh, I can't bear it!'

Averil sighed again, looking with distaste from her frenziedly sobbing sister to her gently sobbing mother.

'Well,' she said, 'if there isn't anything I can do –'

And with that she had quietly and composedly left the room. Which was exactly like Averil.

Altogether a most distressing and painful scene, and one that Joan hadn't thought of for years.

Easily understandable, of course. The sudden shock of their father's illness, and the mystery of the words 'nervous breakdown'. Children always felt better if they could feel a thing was someone's fault. They had made a kind of scapegoat of their mother because she was nearest to hand. Both Tony and Barbara had apologized afterwards. Averil did not seem to think that there was anything for which she needed to apologize, and perhaps, from her own point of view, she was justified. It wasn't the poor child's fault that she really seemed to have been born without any heart.

It had been a difficult, unhappy time altogether while Rodney was away. The children had sulked and been bad tempered. As far as possible they had kept out of her way and that had made her feel curiously lonely. It was, she supposed, the effect of her own sadness and preoccupation. They all loved her dearly, as she knew. Then, too, they were all at difficult ages – Barbara at school still, Averil a gawky and suspicious eighteen. Tony spent most of his time on a neighbouring farm. Annoying that he should have got this silly idea about farming into his head, and very weak of Rodney to have encouraged him. Oh, dear, Joan had thought, it seems too hard that *I* should always have to do all the unpleasant things. When there are such nice girls at Miss Harley's, I really cannot think why Barbara has to make friends with such undesirable specimens. I shall have to make it quite plain to her that she can only bring girls here that I approve of. And then I suppose there will be another row and tears and sulks. Averil, of course, is no help to me, and I do hate that funny sneering way she has of talking. It sounds so badly to outside people.

Yes, thought Joan, bringing up children was a thankless and difficult business.

One didn't really get enough appreciation for it. The tact one had to use, and the good humour. Knowing exactly when to be firm and when to give way. Nobody really knows, thought Joan, what I had to go through that time when Rodney was ill.

Then she winced slightly – for the thought brought up a memory of a remark uttered caustically by Dr McQueen to the effect that during every conversation, sooner or later somebody says, 'Nobody knows what I went through at that time!' Everybody had laughed and said that it was quite true.

Well, thought Joan, wriggling her toes uneasily in her shoes because of the sand that had got in, it's perfectly true. Nobody does know what I went through at that time, not even Rodney.

For when Rodney had come back, in the general relief, everything had swung back to normal, and the children had been their own cheerful, amiable selves again. Harmony had been restored. Which showed, Joan thought, that the whole thing had really been due to anxiety. Anxiety had made her lose her own poise. Anxiety had made the children nervous and bad tempered. A very upsetting time altogether and why she had got to select those particular incidents to think about now – when what she wanted was happy memories and not depressing ones – she really couldn't imagine.

It had all started – what had it started from? Of course – trying to remember poetry. Though really could anything be more ridiculous, thought Joan, than to walk about in a desert spouting poetry! Not that it mattered since there wasn't anybody to see or hear.

There wasn't anybody – no, she adjured herself, no, you must not give way to panic. This is all silliness, sheer nerves . . .

She turned quickly and began to walk back towards the rest house.

She found that she was forcing herself not to break into a run.

There was nothing to be afraid of in being alone – nothing at all. Perhaps she was one of those people who suffered from – now, what was the word? Not claustrophobia, that was the terror of confined spaces – the thing that was the opposite of that. It began with an A. The fear of open spaces.

The whole thing could be explained scientifically.

But explaining it scientifically, though reassuring, didn't at the moment actually help.

Easy to say to yourself that the whole thing was perfectly logical and reasonable, but not so easy to control the curious odds and ends of thoughts that popped in and out of your head for all the world like lizards popping out of holes.

Myrna Randolph, she thought, like a snake – these other things like lizards.

Open spaces – and all her life she'd lived in a box. Yes, a box with toy children and toy servants and a toy husband.

No, Joan, what are you saying – how can you be so silly? Your children are real enough.

The children were real, and so were Cook and Agnes, and so was Rodney. Then perhaps, thought Joan, *I'm* not real. Perhaps I'm just a toy wife and mother.

Oh dear, this was dreadful. Quite incoherent she was getting. Perhaps if she said some more poetry. She must be able to remember *something*.

And aloud, with disproportionate fervour, she exclaimed:

'*From you have I been absent in the Spring.*'

She couldn't remember how it went on. She didn't seem to want to. That line was enough in itself. It explained everything, didn't it? Rodney, she thought, Rodney . . . *From you have I been absent in the Spring*. Only she thought, it's not spring, it's November . . .

And with a sudden sense of shock – But that's what *he* said – that evening . . .

There was a connection there, a clue, a clue to something that was waiting for her, hiding behind the silence. Something from which, she now realized, she wanted to escape.

But how could you escape with lizards popping out of holes all round?

So many things one mustn't let oneself think of. Barbara and Baghdad and Blanche (all Bs, how very curious). And Rodney on the platform at Victoria. And Averil and Tony and Barbara all being so unkind to her.

Really – Joan was exasperated with herself – why didn't she think of the *pleasant* things? So many delightful memories. So many – so very many . . .

Her wedding dress, such a lovely oyster-shell satin . . . Averil in her bassinette, all trimmed with muslin and pink ribbons, such a lovely fair baby and so well behaved. Averil had always been a polite, well-mannered child. 'You bring them up so beautifully, Mrs Scudamore.' Yes, a satisfactory child, Averil – in public, at any rate. In private life given to interminable argument, and with a disconcerting way of looking at you, as though she wondered what you were really like. Not at all the sort of way a child ought to look at its mother. Not, in any sense of the word, a loving child. Tony, too, had always done her credit in public though he was incurably inattentive and vague over things. Barbara was the only difficult child in the family, given to tantrums and storms of tears.

Still, on the whole, they were three very charming, nice-mannered, well brought up children.

A pity children had to grow up and start being difficult.

But she wouldn't think of all that. Concentrate on them in their childhood. Averil at dancing class in her pretty pink silk frock. Barbara in that nice little knitted dress from Liberty's. Tony in those cheery patterned rompers that Nannie made so cleverly –

Somehow, thought Joan, surely she could think of something else except the clothes the children wore! Some charming, affectionate things that they had said to her? Some delightful moments of intimacy?

Considering the sacrifices one made, and the way one did everything for one's children –

Another lizard popping its head out of a hole. Averil

inquiring politely, and with that air of reasonableness that Joan had learned to dread:

'What do you *really* do for us, Mother? You don't *bathe* us, do you?'

'No –'

'And you don't give us our dinners, or brush our hair. Nannie does all that. And she puts us to bed and gets us up. And you don't make our clothes – Nannie does that, too. And she takes us for walks –'

'Yes, dear. I employ Nannie to look after you. That is to say I pay her her wages.'

'I thought Father paid her her wages. Doesn't Father pay for all the things we have?'

'In a way, dear, but it's all the same thing.'

'But *you* don't have to go to the office every morning, only Father. Why don't you have to go to the office?'

'Because I look after the house.'

'But don't Kate and Cook and –'

'That will do, Averil.'

There was one thing to be said for Averil, she always subsided when told. She was never rebellious nor defiant. And yet her submission was often more uncomfortable than rebellion would have been.

Rodney had laughed once and said that with Averil, the verdict was always Non Proven.

'I don't think you ought to laugh, Rodney. I don't think a child of Averil's age ought to be so – so critical.'

'You think she's too young to determine the nature of evidence?'

'Oh, don't be so legal.'

He said, with his teasing smile, 'Who made me into a lawyer?'

'No, but seriously, I think it's disrespectful.'

'I call Averil unusually polite for a child. There's none of the usual devastating frankness children can employ – not like Babs.'

It was true, Joan admitted. Barbara, in one of her states, would shout out, 'You're ugly – you're horrible – I hate you. I wish I was dead. You'd be sorry if I was dead.'

Joan said quickly, 'With Babs it's just temper. And she's always sorry afterwards.'

'Yes, poor little devil. And she doesn't mean what she says. But Averil has got quite a flair for detecting humbug.'

Joan flushed angrily. 'Humbug! I don't know what you mean.'

'Oh, come now, Joan. The stuff we feed them up with. Our assumption of omniscience. The necessity we are under of pretending to do what is best, to know what is best, for those helpless little creatures who are so absolutely in our power.'

'You talk as though they were slaves, not children.'

'Aren't they slaves? They eat the food we give them and wear the clothes we put on them, and say more or less what we tell them to say. It's the price they pay for protection. But every day they live they are growing nearer to freedom.'

'Freedom,' Joan said scornfully. 'Is there any such thing?'

Rodney said slowly and heavily, 'No, I don't think there is. How right you are, Joan . . .'

And he had gone slowly out of the room, his shoulders sagging a little. And she had thought with a sudden pang, I know what Rodney will look like when he is old . . .

Rodney on Victoria platform – the light showing up the lines in his tired face – telling her to take care of herself.

And then, a minute later . . .

Why must she eternally come back to that? It wasn't true! Rodney was missing her a great deal! It was miserable for him in the house alone with the servants! And he probably never thought of asking people in for dinner

– or only somebody stupid like Hargrave Taylor – such a dull man, she never could think why Rodney liked him. Or that tiresome Major Mills who never talked of anything but pasture and cattle breeding . . .

Of course Rodney was missing her!

Chapter Six

She arrived back at the rest house and the Indian came out and asked:

'Memsahib have nice walk?'

Yes, Joan said, she had had a very nice walk.

'Dinner ready soon. Very nice dinner, Memsahib.'

Joan said she was glad of that, but the remark was clearly a ritual one, for dinner was exactly the same as usual, with peaches instead of apricots. It might be a nice dinner, but its disadvantage was that it was always the same dinner.

It was far too early to go to bed when dinner was over and once again Joan wished fervently that she had brought either a large supply of literature or some sewing with her. She even attempted to re-read the more entertaining passages of Lady Catherine Dysart's *Memoirs* but the attempt was a failure.

If there were *anything* to do, Joan thought, anything at *all*! A pack of cards, even. She could have played patience. Or a game – backgammon, chess, draughts – she could have played against herself! *Any* game – halma, snakes and ladders . . .

Really a very curious fancy she had had out there. Lizards popping their heads out of holes. Thoughts popping up out of your mind . . . frightening thoughts, disturbing thoughts . . . thoughts that one didn't want to have.

But if so, why have them? After all one could control one's thoughts – or couldn't one? Was it possible that in some circumstances one's thoughts controlled oneself . . .

popping up out of holes like lizards – or flashing across one's mind like a green snake.

Coming from *somewhere* . . .

Very odd that feeling of panic she had had.

It must be agoraphobia. (Of course that was the word – agoraphobia. It showed that one could always remember things if one only thought hard enough.) Yes, that was it. The terror of open spaces. Curious that she had never known before that she suffered from it. But of course she had never before had any experience of open spaces. She had always lived in the midst of houses and gardens with plenty to do and plenty of people. Plenty of people, that was the thing. If only there was someone here to talk to.

Even Blanche . . .

Funny to think how she had been appalled by the possibility that Blanche might be making the journey home with her.

Why, it would have made all the difference in the world to have had Blanche here. They could have talked over the old days at St Anne's. How very long ago that seemed. What was it Blanche had said? 'You've gone up in the world and I've gone down.' No, she had qualified it afterwards – she had said, 'You've stayed where you were – a St Anne's girl who's been a credit to the school.'

Was there really so little difference in her since those days? Nice to think so. Well, nice in a way, but in another way not so nice. It seemed rather – rather stagnant somehow.

What was it Miss Gilbey had said on the occasion of the leave-taking talk? Miss Gilbey's leave-taking talks to her girls were famous, a recognized institution of St Anne's.

Joan's mind swept back over the years and the figure of her old headmistress loomed immediately into her field of vision with startling clarity. The large, aggressive nose, the pince-nez, the mercilessly sharp eyes with their compelling gaze, the terrific majesty of her progress through the school, slightly preceded by her bust – a restrained, disciplined bust that had about it only majesty and no suggestion of softness.

A terrific figure, Miss Gilbey, justly feared and admired and who could produce just as frightening an effect on parents as on pupils. No denying it, Miss Gilbey *was* St Anne's!

Joan saw herself entering that sacred room, with its flowers, its Medici prints; its implications of culture, scholarship and social graces.

Miss Gilbey, turning majestically from her desk –

'Come in, Joan. Sit down, dear child.'

Joan had sat down as indicated in the cretonne-covered armchair. Miss Gilbey had removed her pince-nez, had produced suddenly an unreal and distinctly terrifying smile.

'You are leaving us, Joan, to go from the circumscribed world of school into the larger world which is life. I should like to have a little talk with you before you go in the hope that some words of mine may be a guide to you in the days that are to come.'

'Yes, Miss Gilbey.'

'Here, in these happy surroundings, with young companions of your own age, you have been shielded from the perplexities and difficulties which no one can entirely avoid in this life.'

'Yes, Miss Gilbey.'

'You have, I know, been happy here.'

'Yes, Miss Gilbey.'

'And you have done well here. I am pleased with the progress you have made. You have been one of our most satisfactory pupils.'

Slight confusion – 'Oh – er – I'm glad, Miss Gilbey.'

'But life opens out before you now with fresh problems, fresh responsibilities –'

The talk flowed on. At the proper intervals Joan murmured:

'Yes, Miss Gilbey.'

She felt slightly hypnotized.

It was one of Miss Gilbey's assets in her career to possess a voice that was, according to Blanche Haggard, orchestral in its compass. Starting with the mellowness of a cello, administering praise in the accents of a flute, deepening to warning in the tones of a bassoon. Then to those girls of marked intellectual prowess the exhortation to a career was proclaimed in terms of brass – to those of more domestic calibre the duties of wifehood and motherhood were mentioned in the muted notes of the violin.

Not until the end of the discourse did Miss Gilbey, as it were, speak pizzicato.

'And now, just a special word. *No lazy thinking*, Joan, my dear! Don't just accept things at their face value – because it's the easiest way, and because it may save you pain! Life is meant to be lived, not glossed over. And don't be too pleased with yourself!'

'Yes – no, Miss Gilbey.'

'Because, just *entre nous*, that *is* a little your failing, isn't it, Joan? Think of others, my dear, and not too much of yourself. And be prepared to accept responsibility.'

And then on to the grand orchestral climax:

'Life, Joan, must be a continual progress – a rising on the stepping stones of our dead selves to higher things. Pain and suffering will come. They come to all. Even Our Lord was not immune from the sufferings of our mortal life. As he knew the agony of Gethsemane, so you will know it – and if you do not know that, Joan, then it will mean that your path has veered far from the true way. Remember this when the hour of doubt and travail comes. And remember, my dear, that I am glad to hear from my old girls at any time – and always ready to help them with advice if they should ask for it. God bless you, dear.'

And thereupon the final benediction of Miss Gilbey's parting kiss, a kiss that was less a human contact than a glorified accolade.

Joan, slightly dazed, was dismissed.

She returned to her dormitory to find Blanche Haggard, wearing Mary Grant's pince-nez, and with a pillow stuffed down the front of her gym tunic, giving an orchestral recital to an enraptured audience:

'You are going,' boomed Blanche, 'from this happy world of school into the larger more perilous world of life. Life opens out before you with its problems, its responsibilities . . .'

Joan joined the audience. The applause grew as Blanche worked up to her climax.

'To you, Blanche Haggard, I say but one word. Discipline. Discipline your emotions, practise self-control. Your very warmth of heart may prove perilous. Only by strict discipline can you attain the heights. You have great gifts, my dear. Use them well. You have a lot of faults, Blanche – a lot of faults. But they are the faults of a generous nature and they can be corrected.

'Life –' Blanche's voice rose to a shrill falsetto, 'is a continual progress. Rise on the stepping stones of our dead selves – (see Wordsworth). Remember the old school and remember that Aunt Gilbey gives advice and help at any time if a stamped addressed envelope is enclosed!'

Blanche paused, but to her surprise neither laughter nor applause greeted the pause. Everyone looked as though turned into marble and all heads were turned to the open doorway where Miss Gilbey stood majestically, pince-nez in hand.

'If you are thinking of taking up a stage career, Blanche, I believe there are several excellent schools of dramatic art where they would teach you proper voice control and elocution. You seem to have some talents in that direction. Kindly return that pillow to its proper place at once.'

And with that she moved swiftly away.

'Whew,' said Blanche. 'The old tartar! Pretty sporting of her – but she does know how to make you feel small.'

Yes, thought Joan, Miss Gilbey had been a great personality. She had finally retired from St Anne's just a term after Averil had been sent there. The new headmistress had lacked her dynamic personality, and the school had started to go down in consequence.

Blanche had been right, Miss Gilbey had been a tartar. But she had known how to make herself felt. And she had certainly, Joan reflected, been quite right about Blanche. Discipline – that was what Blanche had needed in her life. Generous instincts – yes, possibly. But self-control had been notably lacking. Still, Blanche *was* generous. That money, for instance, the money that Joan had sent her – Blanche hadn't spent it on herself. It had bought a roll-top desk for Tom Holliday. A roll-top desk was the last thing in the world that Blanche would have wanted. A warm-hearted kindly creature, Blanche. And yet she had left her children, gone off callously and deserted the two little creatures she herself had brought into the world.

It just showed that there were people who had simply no maternal instinct whatsoever. One's children, thought Joan, should always come first. She and Rodney had always agreed on that. Rodney was really very unselfish – if it was put to him, that is, in the right way. She had pointed out to him, for instance, that that nice sunny dressing-room of his really ought to be the children's day nursery and he had agreed quite willingly to move into the little room overlooking the stable yard. Children should have all the sun and light there was.

She and Rodney had really been very conscientious parents. And the children had really been very satisfactory, especially when they were quite small – such attractive, handsome children. Much better brought up than the

Sherston boys, for instance. Mrs Sherston never seemed to mind what those children looked like. And she herself seemed to join them in the most curious activities, crawling along the ground as a Red Indian – uttering wild whoops and yells – and once when they were attempting a reproduction of a circus, giving a most lifelike imitation of a sea lion!

The fact was, Joan decided, that Leslie Sherston herself had never properly grown up.

Still, she'd had a very sad life, poor woman.

Joan thought of the time when she had so unexpectedly run across Captain Sherston in Somerset.

She had been staying with friends in that part of the world and had had no idea the Sherstons were living there. She had come face to face with Captain Sherston as he emerged (so typical) from the local pub.

She had not seen him since his release and it was really quite a shock to see the difference from the old days of the jaunty, confident bank manager.

That curiously deflated look that big aggressive men got when they had failed in the world. The sagging shoulders, the loose waistcoat, the flabby cheeks, the quick shifty look of the eyes.

To think that anyone could ever have trusted this man.

He was taken aback by meeting her, but he rallied well, and greeted her with what was a painful travesty of his old manner:

'Well, well, well, Mrs Scudamore! The world is indeed a small place. And what brings you to Skipton Haynes?'

Standing there, squaring his shoulders, endeavouring to put into his voice the old heartiness and self assurance. It was a pitiful performance and Joan had, in spite of herself, felt quite sorry for him.

How dreadful to come down in the world like that! To feel that at any moment you might come across someone from the old life, someone who might refuse even to recognize you.

Not that she had any intention herself of behaving that way. Naturally she was quite prepared to be kind.

Sherston was saying, 'You must come back and see my wife. You must have tea with us. Yes, yes, dear lady, I insist!'

And the parody of his old manner was so painful that Joan, albeit rather unwillingly, allowed herself to be piloted along the street, Sherston continuing to talk in his new uneasy way.

He'd like her to see their little place – at least not so little. Quite a good acreage. Hard work, of course, growing for the market. Anemones and apples were their best line.

Still talking he unlatched a somewhat dilapidated gate that needed painting and they walked up a weedy drive. Then they saw Leslie, her back bent over the anemone beds.

'Look who's here,' Sherston called and Leslie had pushed her hair back from her face and had come over and said this *was* a surprise!

Joan had noticed at once how much older Leslie looked and how ill. There were lines carved by fatigue and pain on her face. But, otherwise, she was exactly the same as usual, cheerful and untidy and terrifically energetic.

As they were standing there talking, the boys arrived home from school, charging up the drive with loud howls and rushing at Leslie, butting at her with their heads, shouting out Mum, Mum, Mum, and Leslie after enduring the onslaught for some minutes suddenly said in a very peremptory voice, 'Quiet! Visitors.'

And the boys had suddenly transformed themselves into two polite angels who shook hands with Mrs Scudamore, and spoke in soft hushed voices.

Joan was reminded a little of a cousin of hers who

trained sporting dogs. On the word of command the dogs would sit, dropping to their haunches, or on another word dash wildly for the horizon. Leslie's children, she thought, seemed trained much on the same plan.

They went into the house and Leslie went to get tea with the boys helping her and presently it came in on a tray, with the loaf and the butter and the homemade jam, and the thick kitchen cups and Leslie and the boys laughing.

But the most curious thing that happened was the change in Sherston. That uneasy, shifty, painful manner of his vanished. He became suddenly the master of the house and the host – and a very good host. Even his social manner was in abeyance. He looked suddenly happy, pleased with himself and with his family. It was as though, within these four walls, the outer world and its judgment ceased to exist for him. The boys clamoured for him to help them with some carpentry they were doing, Leslie adjured him not to forget that he had promised to see to the hoe for her and ought they to bunch the anemones tomorrow or could they do it Thursday morning?

Joan thought to herself that she had never liked him better. She understood, she felt, for the first time Leslie's devotion to him. Besides, he must have been a very good-looking man once.

But a moment or two later she got rather a shock.

Peter was crying eagerly, 'Tell us the funny story about the warder and the plum pudding!'

And then, urgently, as his father looked blank:

'*You* know, when you were in prison, what the warder said, and the other warder?'

Sherston hesitated and looked slightly shamefaced. Leslie's voice said calmly:

'Go on, Charles. It's a very funny story. Mrs Scudamore would like to hear it.'

So he had told it, and it was quite funny – if not so

funny as the boys seemed to think. They rolled about squirming and gasping with laughter. Joan laughed politely, but she was definitely startled and a little shocked, and later, when Leslie had taken her upstairs she murmured delicately:

'I'd no idea – they *knew*!'

Leslie – really, Joan thought, Leslie Sherston must be most insensitive – looked rather amused.

'They'd be bound to know some day,' she said. 'Wouldn't they? So they might just as well know now. It's simpler.'

It was simpler, Joan agreed, but was it wise? The delicate idealism of a child's mind, to shatter its trust and faith – she broke off.

Leslie said she didn't think her children were very delicate and idealistic. It would be worse for them, she thought, to know there was something – and not be told what it was.

She waved her hands in that clumsy, inarticulate way she had and said, 'Making mysteries – all that – *much* worse. When they asked me why Daddy had gone away I thought I might just as well be natural about it, so I told them that he'd stolen money from the bank and gone to prison. After all, they know what stealing is. Peter used to steal jam and get sent to bed for it. If grown-up people do things that are wrong they get sent to prison. It's quite simple.'

'All the same, for a child to look *down* on its father instead of *up* to him –'

'Oh they don't look down on him.' Leslie again seemed amused. 'They're actually quite sorry for him – and they love to hear all about the prison life.'

'I'm sure that's *not* a good thing,' said Joan decidedly.

'Oh don't you think so?' Leslie meditated. 'Perhaps not. But it's been good for Charles. He came back simply cringing – like a dog. I couldn't bear it. So I thought the only thing to do was to be quite natural about it. After all, you can't pretend three years of your life have never existed. It's better, I think, to treat it as just one of those things.'

And that, thought, Joan, was Leslie Sherston, casual, slack, and with no conception of any finer shades of feeling! Always taking the way of least resistance.

Still, give her her due, she had been a loyal wife.

Joan had said kindly, 'You know, Leslie, I really think you have been quite splendid, the way you have stuck to your husband and worked so hard to keep things going while he was – er – away. Rodney and I often say so.'

What a funny one-sided smile the woman had. Joan hadn't noticed it until this minute. Perhaps her praise had embarrassed Leslie. It was certainly in rather a stiff voice that Leslie asked:

'How is – Rodney?'

'Very busy, the poor lamb. I'm always telling him he ought to take a day off now and again.'

Leslie said, 'That's not so easy. I suppose in his job – like mine – it's pretty well full time. There aren't many possible days off.'

'No. I daresay that's true, and of course Rodney is very conscientious.'

'A full-time job,' Leslie said. She went slowly towards the window and stood there staring out.

Something about the outline of her figure struck Joan – Leslie usually wore things pretty shapeless, but surely –

'Oh Leslie,' Joan exclaimed impulsively. 'Surely you aren't –'

Leslie turned and meeting the other woman's eyes slowly nodded her head.

'Yes,' she said. 'In August.'

'Oh my dear.' Joan felt genuinely distressed.

And suddenly, surprisingly, Leslie broke into passionate speech. She was no longer casual and slack. She was like a condemned prisoner who puts up a defence.

'It's made all the difference to Charles. All the difference! Do you see? I can't tell you how he feels about it. It's a kind of symbol – that he's not an outcast – that everything's the same as it always was. He's even tried to stop drinking since he's known.'

So impassioned was Leslie's voice that Joan hardly realized until afterwards the implication of the last sentence.

She said, 'Of course you know your own business best, but I should have thought it was unwise – at the moment.'

'Financially, you mean?' Leslie laughed. 'Oh we'll weather the storm. We grow pretty well all we eat anyway.'

'And, you know, you don't look very strong.'

'Strong? I'm terribly strong. Too strong. Whatever kills me won't kill me easily, I'm afraid.'

And she had given a little shiver – as though – even then – she had had some strange prevision of disease and racking pain . . .

And then they had gone downstairs again, and Sherston had said he would walk with Mrs Scudamore to the corner and show her the short cut across the fields, and, turning her head as they went down the drive, she saw Leslie and the boys all tangled up and rolling over and over on the ground with shrieks of wild mirth. Leslie, rolling about with her young, quite like an animal, thought Joan with slight disgust, and then bent her head attentively to listen to what Captain Sherston was saying.

He was saying in rather incoherent terms that there never was, never had been, never would be, any woman like his wife.

'You've no idea, Mrs Scudamore, what she's been to me. No idea. Nobody could. I'm not worthy of her. I know that . . .'

Joan observed with alarm that the easy tears were

standing in his eyes. He was a man who could quickly become maudlin.

'Always the same – always cheerful – seems to think that everything that happens is interesting and amusing. And never a word of reproach. Never a word. But I'll make it up to her – I swear I'll make it up to her.'

It occurred to Joan that Captain Sherston could best show his appreciation by not visiting the Anchor and Bell too frequently. She very nearly said so.

She got away from him at last, saying, Of course, of course, and what he said was *so* true, and it had been so nice to see them both. She went away across the fields and looking back as she crossed the stile, she saw Captain Sherston at a standstill outside the Anchor and Bell, looking at his watch to decide how long it was to opening time.

The whole thing, she said to Rodney, when she got back, was very sad.

And Rodney, seemingly purposefully dense, had said, 'I thought you said that they all seemed very happy together?'

'Well, yes, in a way.'

Rodney said that it seemed to him as though Leslie Sherston was making quite a success of a bad business.

'She's certainly being very plucky about it all. And just think – she's actually going to have another child.'

Rodney had got up on that and walked slowly across to the window. He had stood there looking out – very much, now she came to think of it, as Leslie had stood. He said, after a minute or two, 'When?'

'August,' she said. 'I think it's extremely foolish of her.'

'Do you?'

'My dear, just consider. They're living hand to mouth as it is. A young baby will be an added complication.'

He said slowly, 'Leslie's shoulders are broad.'

'Well, she'll crack up if she tries to take on too much. She looks ill now.'

'She looked ill when she left here.'

'She looks years older, too. It's all very well to say that this will make all the difference to Charles Sherston.'

'Is that what she said?'

'Yes. She said it *had* made all the difference.'

Rodney said thoughtfully, 'That's probably true. Sherston is one of those extraordinary people who live entirely on the esteem in which other people hold them. When the judge passed sentence on him he collapsed just like a pricked balloon. It was quite pitiful and at the same time quite disgusting. I should say the only hope for Sherston is to get back, somehow or other, his self respect. It will be a full-time job.'

'Still I really do think that another child –'

Rodney interrupted her. He turned from the window and the white anger of his face startled her.

'She's his wife, isn't she? She'd only got two courses open to her – to cut loose entirely and take the kids – or to go back and damn well *be* a wife to him. That's what she's done – and Leslie doesn't do things by halves.'

And Joan had asked if there was anything to get excited about and Rodney replied, 'Certainly not,' but he was sick and tired of a prudent, careful world that counted the cost of everything before doing it and never took a risk! Joan said she hoped he didn't talk like that to his clients, and Rodney grinned and said, No fear, he always advised them to settle out of court!

Chapter Seven

It was, perhaps, natural that Joan should dream that night of Miss Gilbey. Miss Gilbey in a solar topee, walking beside her in the desert and saying in an authoritative voice, 'You should have paid more attention to lizards, Joan. Your natural history is weak.' To which, of course, she had replied, 'Yes, Miss Gilbey.'

And Miss Gilbey had said, 'Now don't pretend you don't know what I mean, Joan. You know perfectly well. Discipline, my dear.'

Joan woke up and for a moment or two thought herself back at St Anne's. It was true the rest house was not unlike a school dormitory. The bareness, the iron beds, the rather hygienic-looking walls.

Oh dear, thought Joan, another day to get through.

What was it Miss Gilbey had said in her dream? 'Discipline.'

Well, there was something in that. It had really been very foolish of her the day before to get into that queer state all about nothing! She must discipline her thoughts, arrange her mind systematically – investigate once and for all this agoraphobia idea.

Certainly she felt quite all right now, here in the rest house. Perhaps it would be wiser not to go out at all?

But her heart sank at the prospect. All day in the gloom, with the smell of mutton fat and paraffin and Flit – all day with nothing to read – nothing to do.

What did prisoners do in their cells? Well, of course they had exercise and they sewed mail bags or something like that. Otherwise, she supposed, they would go mad.

But there was solitary confinement . . . that did send people mad.

Solitary confinement – day after day – week after week.

Why, she felt as though she had been here for *weeks*! And it was – how long – two days?

Two days! Incredible. What was that line of Omar Khayyam's? 'Myself with Yesterday's Ten Thousand Years.' Something like that. Why couldn't she remember anything properly?

No, no, not again. Trying to remember and recite poetry hadn't been a success – not at all a success. The truth is there was something very upsetting about poetry. It had a poignancy – a way of striking through to the spirit . . .

What was she talking about? Surely the more spiritual one's thoughts were the better. And she had always been a rather spiritual type of person . . .

'*You always were as cold as a fish . . .*'

Why should Blanche's voice come cutting through to her thoughts? A very vulgar and uncalled for remark – really, just like Blanche! Well, she supposed that that was what it must seem like to someone like Blanche, someone who allowed themselves to be torn to pieces by their passions. You couldn't really blame Blanche for being coarse – she was simply made that way. It hadn't been noticeable as a girl because she had been so lovely and so well bred, but the coarseness must always have been there underneath.

Cold as a fish indeed! Nothing of the kind.

It would have been a good deal better for Blanche if *she* had been a little more fishlike in temperament herself!

She seemed to have led the most deplorable life.

Really *quite* deplorable.

What had she said? 'One can always think of one's sins!'

Poor Blanche! But she had admitted that that wouldn't

give Joan occupation long. She did realize, then, the difference between herself and Joan. She had pretended to think that Joan would soon get tired of counting her blessings. (True, perhaps, that one did tend to take one's blessings for granted!) What was it she had said after that? Something rather curious . . .

Oh yes. She had wondered what, if you had nothing to do but think about yourself for days and days, you might find out about yourself . . .

In a way, rather an interesting idea.

In fact, quite an interesting idea.

Only Blanche had said that she, herself, wouldn't like to try it . . .

She had sounded – almost – *afraid*.

I wonder, thought Joan, if one *would* make any discoveries about oneself.

Of course I'm not *used* to thinking of myself . . .

I've never been a self-centred sort of woman.

. . . I wonder, thought Joan, how I appear to other people?

. . . I don't mean in general – I mean in particular.

She tried to remember any instances of things people had said to her . . .

Barbara, for instance:

'Oh, *your* servants, Mother, are always perfection. *You* see to that.'

Quite a tribute, in a way, showing that her children did consider her a good manager and housewife. And it was true, she did run her house well and efficiently. And her servants liked her – at least, they did what she told them. They weren't, perhaps, very sympathetic if she had a headache, or wasn't feeling well, but then she hadn't encouraged them on those lines. And what was it that that very excellent cook had said when she had given her notice, something about not being able to go on for ever without any appreciation – something quite ridiculous.

'Always being told when a thing's wrong, Ma'am, and never a word of praise when it's right – well, it takes the heart out of you.'

She had answered coldly, 'Surely you realize, Cook, that if nothing is said it is because everything is all right and perfectly satisfactory.'

'That may be, Ma'am, but it's disheartening. After all, I'm a human being – and I did take a lot of trouble over that Spanish Ragout you asked for, though it was a lot of trouble and I'm not one that cares for made-up dishes myself.'

'It was quite excellent, Cook.'

'Yes, Ma'am. I thought it must have been as you finished it all in the dining-room, but nothing was said.'

Joan said impatiently, 'Don't you think you are being rather silly? After all, you are engaged to do the cooking at a very good salary –'

'Oh, the wages are quite satisfactory, Ma'am.'

'– and therefore the understanding is that you are a sufficiently good cook. If anything is *not* satisfactory, I mention it.'

'You do indeed, Ma'am.'

'And apparently you resent the fact?'

'It's not that, Ma'am, but I think we'd best say no more about it and I'll leave at the end of my month.'

Servants, thought Joan, were very unsatisfactory. So full of feelings and resentments. They all adored Rodney, of course, simply because he was a man. Nothing was ever too much trouble to do for the Master. And Rodney would sometimes come out with the most unexpected knowledge concerning them.

'Don't pitch into Edna,' he would say surprisingly. 'Her young man's taken up with another girl and it's thrown her right out of gear. That's why she's dropping things and handing the vegetables twice and forgetting everything.'

'How on earth do you know, Rodney?'

'She told me this morning.'

'Very extraordinary that she should talk to *you* about it.'

'Well, I asked her what was wrong, as a matter of fact. I noticed her eyes were red as though she had been crying.'

Rodney, thought Joan, was an unusually kind person.

She had said to him once, 'I should think that with your experience as a lawyer, you would get tired of human tangles.'

And he had answered, thoughtfully, 'Yes, one might think so. But it doesn't work that way. I suppose a country family solicitor sees more of the seamy side of human relationships than almost anybody else, except a doctor. But it only seems to deepen one's pity for the whole human race – so vulnerable, so prone to fear and suspicion and greed – and sometimes so unexpectedly unselfish and brave. That is, perhaps, the only compensation there is – the widening of one's sympathies.'

It had been on the tip of her tongue to say, 'Compensation? What do you mean?' But for some reason she hadn't said it. Better not, she thought. No, better to say nothing.

But she had been disturbed sometimes by the practical expression of Rodney's easily awakened sympathies.

The question, for instance, of old Hoddesdon's mortgage.

She had learned about that, not from Rodney, but from the garrulous wife of Hoddesdon's nephew, and she had come home seriously perturbed.

Was it true that Rodney had advanced the money out of his private capital?

Rodney had looked vexed. He had flushed and answered heatedly:

'Who's been talking?'

She told him and then said, 'Why couldn't he borrow the money in the ordinary way?'

'Security isn't good enough from the strictly business point of view. It's difficult to raise mortgages on farmland just now.'

'Then why on earth are *you* lending it?'

'Oh, I shall be all right. Hoddesdon's a good farmer really. It's lack of capital and two bad seasons that have let him down.'

'The fact remains that he's in a bad way and has to raise money. I really can't feel that this is good business, Rodney.'

And quite suddenly and unexpectedly, Rodney had lost his temper.

Did she understand the first thing, he had asked her, about the plight that farmers all over the country were in? Did she realize the difficulties, the obstacles, the short-sighted policy of the Government? He had stood there pouring out a welter of information concerning the whole agricultural position of England, passing from that to a warm, indignant description of old Hoddesdon's particular difficulties.

'It might happen to anyone. No matter how intelligent and hard-working he was. It might have happened to me if I'd been in his position. It's lack of capital to begin with and bad luck following on. And anyway, if you don't mind my saying so, it isn't your business, Joan. I don't interfere with your management of the house and the children. That's your department. This is mine.'

She had been hurt – quite bitterly hurt. To take such a tone was most unlike Rodney. It was really the nearest they had come to having a quarrel.

And all over that tiresome old Hoddesdon. Rodney was besotted about the stupid old man. On Sunday afternoons he would go out there and spend the afternoon walking round with Hoddesdon and come back full of information about the state of the crops and cattle diseases and other totally uninteresting subjects of conversation.

He even used to victimize their guests with the same kind of talk.

Why, Joan remembered how at a garden party she had noticed Rodney and Mrs Sherston sitting together on one of the garden seats, with Rodney talking, talking, talking. So much so that she had wondered what on earth he had been talking about and had gone up to them. Because really he seemed so excited, and Leslie Sherston was listening with such apparently tense interest.

And apparently all he was talking about were dairy herds and the necessity of keeping up the level of pedigree stock in this country.

Hardly a subject that could be of any interest to Leslie Sherston, who had no particular knowledge of or interest in such matters. Yet she had been listening with apparently deep attention, her eyes on Rodney's eager, animated face.

Joan had said lightly, 'Really, Rodney, you mustn't bore poor Mrs Sherston with such dull things.' (For that had been where the Sherstons first came to Crayminster and before they knew them very well.)

The light had died out of Rodney's face and he had said apologetically to Leslie:

'I'm sorry.'

And Leslie Sherston had said quickly and abruptly, in the way she always spoke:

'You're wrong, Mrs Scudamore. I found what Mr Scudamore was saying very interesting.'

And there had been a gleam in her eye which had made Joan say to herself, 'Really, I believe that woman has got quite a temper . . .'

And the next thing that had happened was that Myrna Randolph had come up, just a little out of breath, and had exclaimed:

'Rodney darling, you must come and play in this set with *me*. We're waiting for you.'

And with that charming imperious manner that only a really good-looking girl can get away with, she had stretched out both hands, pulled Rodney to his feet and smiling up into his face, had simply swept him away to the tennis court. Whether Rodney had wanted to or not!

She had walked beside him, her arm familiarly slipped through his, turning her head, gazing up into his face.

And Joan had thought angrily to herself, It's all very well, but men don't like girls who throw themselves at their heads like that.

And then had wondered, with a sudden queer cold feeling, whether perhaps men *did* like it after all!

She had looked up to find Leslie Sherston watching her. Leslie no longer looked as though she had a temper. She looked, instead, as though she was rather sorry for her, Joan. Which was impertinence if nothing else.

Joan stirred restlessly in her narrow bed. How on earth had she got back to Myrna Randolph? Oh, of course, wondering what effect she herself had on other people. Myrna, she supposed, had disliked her. Well, Myrna was welcome to do so. The kind of girl who would break up anybody's married life if she got the chance!

Well, well, no need getting hot and bothered about that now.

She must get up and have breakfast. Perhaps they could poach an egg for her as a change? She was so tired of leathery omelettes.

The Indian, however, seemed impervious to the suggestion of a poached egg.

'Cook egg in water? You mean boil?'

No, Joan said, she didn't mean boil. A boiled egg in the rest house, as she knew by experience, was always hard boiled. She tried to explain the science of the poached egg. The Indian shook his head.

'Put egg in water – egg all go away. I give Memsahib nice fried egg.'

So Joan had two nice fried eggs, well frizzled outside and with hard, firm pale yolks. On the whole, she thought, she preferred the omelette.

Breakfast was over all too soon. She inquired for news of the train, but there was no news.

So there she was fairly and squarely up against it. Another long day ahead of her.

But today, at any rate, she would plan her time out intelligently. The trouble was that up to now she had just tried to pass the time.

She had been a person waiting at a railway station for a train, and naturally that engendered in one a nervy, jumpy frame of mind.

Supposing she were to consider this as a period of rest and – yes, *discipline*. Something in the nature of a Retreat. That is what Roman Catholics called it. They went for Retreats and came back spiritually refreshed.

There is no reason, thought Joan, why I should not be spiritually refreshed too.

Her life had been, perhaps, too slack lately. Too pleasant, too easy going.

A wraithlike Miss Gilbey seemed to be standing at her side and saying, in the well-remembered bassoon-like accents, 'Discipline!'

Only actually that was what she had said to Blanche Haggard. To Joan she had said (really rather unkindly), '*Don't be too pleased with yourself, Joan.*'

It was unkind. For Joan never had been in the least bit pleased with herself – not in that fatuous sort of way. '*Think of others, my dear, and not too much of yourself.*' Well, that is what she had done – always thought of others. She hardly ever thought of herself – or put herself first. She had always been unselfish – thinking of the children – of Rodney.

Averil!

Why did she have suddenly to think of Averil?

Why see so clearly her elder daughter's face – with its polite, slightly scornful smile.

Averil, there was no doubt of it, had never appreciated her mother properly.

The things she said sometimes, quite sarcastic things, were really most irritating. Not exactly rude, but –

Well, but what?

That look of quiet amusement, those raised eyebrows. The way Averil would stroll gently out of a room.

Averil was devoted to her, of course, all her children were devoted to her –

Were they?

Were her children devoted to her – did they really care for her at all?

Joan half rose out of her chair, then sank back.

Where did these ideas come from? What made her think them? Such frightening, unpleasant ideas. Put them out of her head – try not to think of them . . .

Miss Gilbey's voice – *pizzicato* –

'*No lazy thinking, Joan. Don't accept things at their face value, because that's the easiest way, and because it may save you pain . . .*'

Was that why she wanted to force these ideas back? To save herself pain?

Because they certainly were painful ideas . . .

Averil . . .

Was Averil devoted to her? *Was* Averil – come now, Joan, face it – was Averil even *fond* of her?

Well, the truth was that Averil was rather a peculiar kind of girl – cool, unemotional.

No, not perhaps unemotional. Actually Averil had been the only one of the three children to give them real trouble.

Cool, well-behaved, quiet Averil. The shock it had given them!

The shock it had given *her*!

She had opened the letter without the least suspicion of its contents. Addressed in a scrawled, illiterate hand, she had taken it to be from one of her many charitable pensioners.

She had read the words almost uncomprehendingly.

'This is to let you know as how your eldest daughter is carrying on with the Dr up at the Saniturum. Kissing in the woods something shameful it is and ought to be stopped.'

Joan stared at the dirty sheet of paper with a definite feeling of nausea.

What an abominable – what a disgusting – thing –

She had heard of anonymous letters. She had never received one before. Really, it made one feel quite sick.

Your eldest daughter – Averil? Averil of all people in the world? *Carrying on* (disgusting phrase) *with the Dr up at the Saniturum*. Dr Cargill? That eminent, distinguished specialist who had made such a success of his tubercular treatment, a man at least twenty years older than Averil, a man with a charming invalid wife.

What rubbish! What disgusting rubbish.

And at that moment, Averil herself had walked into the room and had asked, but with only mild curiosity, for Averil was never really curious, 'Is anything the matter, Mother?'

Joan, the hand that held the letter shaking, had hardly been able to reply.

'I don't think I had better even show it to you, Averil. It's – it's too disgusting.'

Her voice had trembled. Averil, raising those cool, delicate eyebrows of hers in surprise, said, 'Something in a letter?'

'Yes.'

'About me?'

'You'd better not even see it, dear.'

But Averil, walking across the room, had quietly taken the letter out of her hand.

Had stood there a minute reading it, then had handed it back, and had said in a reflective, detached voice, 'Yes, not very nice.'

'Nice? It's disgusting – quite disgusting. People should be punished by law for telling such lies.'

Averil said quietly, 'It's a foul letter, but it's not a lie.'

The room had turned a somersault and revolved round and round. Joan had gasped out:

'What do you mean – what can you mean?'

'You needn't make such a fuss, Mother. I'm sorry this has come to you this way, but I suppose you would have been bound to know sooner or later.'

'You mean it's *true*? That *you* and – and Dr Cargill –'

'Yes.' Averil had just nodded her head.

'But it's wicked – it's disgraceful. A man of that age, a married man – and a young girl like you –'

Averil said impatiently, 'You needn't make a kind of village melodrama out of it. It's not in the least like that. It's all happened very gradually. Rupert's wife is an invalid – has been for years. We've – well, we've simply come to care for each other. That's all.'

'That's all, indeed!' Joan had plenty to say, and said it. Averil merely shrugged her shoulders and let the storm play round her. In the end, when Joan had exhausted herself, Averil remarked:

'I can quite appreciate your point of view, Mother. I daresay I should feel the same in your place – though I don't think I should have said some of the things you've chosen to say. But you can't alter facts. Rupert and I care for each other. And although I'm sorry, I really don't see what you can do about it.'

'Do about it? I shall speak to your father – at once.'

'Poor Father. Must you really worry him about it?'

'I'm sure he'll know just what to do.'

'He really can't do anything at all. And it will simply worry him dreadfully.'

That had been the beginning of a really shattering time.

Averil, at the heart of the storm, had remained cool and apparently unperturbed.

But also completely obdurate.

Joan had repeated to Rodney again and again, 'I can't help feeling it's all a *pose* on her part. It's not as though Averil were given to really strong feeling of any kind.'

But Rodney had shaken his head.

'You don't understand Averil. With Averil it is less her senses than her mind and heart. When she loves, she loves so deeply that I doubt if she will ever quite get over it.'

'Oh, Rodney, I really do think that is nonsense! After all, I know Averil better than you do. I'm her mother.'

'That doesn't mean that you really know the least thing about her. Averil has always understated things from choice – no, perhaps from necessity. Feeling a thing deeply she belittles it purposely in words.'

'That sounds very far-fetched to me.'

Rodney said slowly, 'Well, you can take it from me that it isn't. It's true.'

'I can't help thinking that you are exaggerating what is simply a silly schoolgirl flirtation. She's been flattered and likes to imagine –'

Rodney had interrupted her.

'Joan, my dear – it's no good trying to reassure yourself by saying things that you yourself don't believe. Averil's passion for Cargill is serious.'

'Then it's disgraceful of *him* – absolutely disgraceful . . .'

'Yes, that's what the world will say all right. But put yourself in the poor devil's place. A wife who's a permanent invalid and all the passion and beauty of Averil's young, generous heart offered to you on a platter. All the eagerness and freshness of her mind.'

'Twenty years older than she is!'

'I know, I know. If he were only ten years younger the temptation wouldn't be so great.'

'He must be a horrid man – perfectly horrid.'

Rodney sighed.

'He's not. He's a fine and very humane man – a man with an intense enthusiastic love for his profession – a man who has done outstanding work. Incidentally, a man who has always been unvaryingly kind and gentle to an ailing wife.'

'Now you are trying to make him out a kind of saint.'

'Far from it. And most saints, Joan, have had their passions. They were seldom bloodless men and women. No, Cargill's human enough. Human enough to fall in love and to suffer. Human enough, probably, to wreck his own life – and to nullify his lifework. It all depends.'

'Depends on what?'

Rodney said slowly, 'It depends on our daughter. On how strong she is – and how clear-sighted.'

Joan said energetically, 'We must get her away from here. How about sending her on a cruise? To the northern capitals – or the Greek Islands? Something like that.'

Rodney smiled.

'Aren't you thinking of the treatment applied to your old school friend, Blanche Haggard? It didn't work very well in her case, remember.'

'Do you mean that Averil would come rushing back from some foreign port?'

'I rather doubt whether Averil would even start.'

'Nonsense. We would insist.'

'Joan dear, do try and envisage realities. You cannot apply force to an adult young woman. We can neither lock Averil in her bedroom nor force her to leave Crayminster – and actually I don't want to do either. Those things are only palliatives. Averil can only be influenced by factors that she respects.'

'And those are?'

'Reality. Truth.'

'Why don't you go to him – to Rupert Cargill. Threaten him with the scandal.'

Again Rodney sighed.

'I'm afraid, terribly afraid, Joan, of precipitating matters.'

'What do you mean?'

'That Cargill will throw up everything and that they will go away together.'

'Wouldn't that be the end of his career?'

'Undoubtedly. I don't suppose it would come under the heading of unprofessional conduct, but it would completely alienate public opinion in his special circumstances.'

'Then surely, if he realizes that –'

Rodney said impatiently, 'He's not quite sane at the moment. Don't you understand anything at all about love, Joan?'

Which was a ridiculous question to ask! She said bitterly:

'Not *that* kind of love, I'm thankful to say . . .'

And then Rodney had taken her quite by surprise. He had smiled at her, had said, 'Poor little Joan' very gently, had kissed her and had gone quietly away.

It was nice of him, she thought, to realize how unhappy she was over the whole miserable business.

Yes, it had indeed been an anxious time. Averil silent, not speaking to anybody – sometimes not even replying when her mother spoke to her.

I did my best, thought Joan. But what are you to do with a girl who won't even listen?

Pale, wearily polite, Averil would say:

'Really, Mother, must we go on like this? Talking

and talking and talking? I do make allowances for your point of view, but won't you just accept the plain truth, that nothing you can say or do will make the least difference?'

So it had gone on, until that afternoon in September when Averil, her face a little paler than usual, had said to them both:

'I think I'd better tell you. Rupert and I don't feel we can go on like this any longer. We are going away together. I hope his wife will divorce him. But if she won't it makes no difference.'

Joan had started on an energetic protest, but Rodney had stopped her.

'Leave this to me, Joan, if you don't mind. Averil, I must talk to you. Come into my study.'

Averil had said with a very faint smile, 'Quite like a headmaster, aren't you, Father.'

Joan burst out, 'I'm Averil's mother, I insist –'

'Please, Joan. I want to talk to Averil alone. Would you mind leaving us?'

There had been so much quiet decision in his tone that she had half turned to leave the room. It was Averil's low, clear voice that stopped her.

'Don't go away, Mother. I don't want you to go away. Anything Father says to me I'd rather he said in front of you.'

Well, at least that showed, thought Joan, that being a mother had some importance.

What a very odd way Averil and her father had of looking at each other, a wary, measuring, unfriendly way, like two antagonists on the stage.

Then Rodney smiled slightly and said, 'I see. *Afraid!*'

Averil's answer came cool and slightly surprised, 'I don't know what you mean, Father.'

Rodney said, with sudden irrelevance, 'A pity you weren't a boy, Averil. There are times when you are quite uncannily like your Great-Uncle Henry. He had a wonderful eye for the best way to conceal the weakness in his own case, or to expose the weakness of his opponent's case.'

Averil said quickly, 'There isn't any weakness in my case.'

Rodney said deliberately, 'I shall prove to you that there is.'

Joan exclaimed sharply, 'Of course you are not going to do anything so wicked or so foolish, Averil. Your father and I will not allow it.'

And at that Averil had smiled just a little and had looked not at her mother, but at her father, offering as it were her mother's remark to him.

Rodney said, 'Please, Joan, leave this to me.'

'I think,' said Averil, 'that Mother is perfectly entitled to say just what she thinks.'

'Thank you, Averil,' said Joan. 'I am certainly going to do so. My dear child, you must see that what you propose is quite out of the question. You are young and romantic and you see everything in quite a false light. What you do on an impulse now you will bitterly regret later. And think of the sorrow you will cause your father and me. Have you thought of that? I'm sure you don't want to cause us pain – we have always loved you so dearly.'

Averil listened quite patiently, but she did not reply. She had never taken her eyes from her father's face.

When Joan finished, Averil was still looking at Rodney and there was still a faint, slightly mocking smile on her lips.

'Well, Father,' she said. 'Have you anything to add?'

'Not to add,' said Rodney. 'But I have something of my own to say.'

Averil looked at him inquiringly.

'Averil,' said Rodney, 'do you understand exactly what a marriage is?'

Averil's eyes opened slightly. She paused and then said, 'Are you telling me that it is a sacrament?'

'No,' said Rodney. '*I* may consider it as a sacrament, or I may not. What I am telling *you* is that marriage is a *contract*.'

'Oh,' said Averil.

She seemed a little, just a little, taken aback.

'Marriage,' said Rodney, 'is a contract entered into by two people, both of adult years, in the full possession of their faculties, and with a full knowledge of what they are undertaking. It is a specification of partnership, and each partner binds himself and herself specifically to honour the terms of that contract – that is, to stand by each other in certain eventualities – in sickness and in health, for richer for poorer, for better for worse.

'Because those words are uttered in a church, and with the approval and benediction of a priest, they are none the less a contract, just as any agreement entered into between two people in good faith is a contract. Because some of the obligations undertaken are not enforcible in a court of law, they are none the less binding on the persons who have assumed them. I think you will agree that, equitably, that is so.'

There was a pause and then Avril said, 'That may have been true once. But marriage is looked upon differently nowadays and a great many people are not married in church and do not use the words of the church service.'

'That may be so. But eighteen years ago Rupert Cargill did bind himself by using those words in a church, and I challenge you to say that he did not, at that time, utter those words in good faith and meaning to carry them out.'

Averil shrugged her shoulders.

Rodney said, 'Will you admit that, although not legally enforcible, Rupert Cargill did enter into such a contract with the woman who is his wife? He envisaged, at the time, the possibilities of poverty and of sickness, and directly specified them as not affecting the permanence of the bond.'

Averil had gone very white. She said, 'I don't know where you think you are getting by all this.'

'I want an admission from you that marriage is, apart from all sentimental feeling and thinking, an ordinary business contract. Do you admit that, or don't you?'

'I'll admit it.'

'And Rupert Cargill proposes to break that contract with your connivance?'

'Yes.'

'With no regard for the due rights and privileges of the other party to the contract?'

'She will be all right. It's not as though she were so terribly fond of Rupert. All she thinks of is her own health and –'

Rodney interrupted her sharply, 'I don't want sentiment from you, Averil. I want an admission of *fact*.'

'I'm not sentimental.'

'You are. You have no knowledge at all of Mrs Cargill's thoughts and feelings. You are imagining them to suit yourself. All I want from you is the admission that she has *rights*.'

Averil flung her head back.

'Very well. She has rights.'

'Then you are now quite clear exactly what it is you are doing?'

'Have you finished, Father?'

'No, I have one more thing to say. You realize, don't you, that Cargill is doing very valuable and important work, that his methods in treating tuberculosis have met with such striking success that he is a very prominent figure in the medical world, and that, unfortunately, a man's private affairs can affect his public career. That means that Cargill's work, his usefulness to humanity, will be seriously affected, if not destroyed, by what you are both proposing to do.'

Averil said, 'Are you trying to persuade me that it's my duty to give Rupert up so that he can continue to benefit humanity?'

There was a faint sneer in her voice.

'No,' said Rodney. 'I'm thinking of the poor devil himself . . .'

There was sudden vehement feeling in his voice.

'You can take it from me, Averil, that a man who's not doing the work he wants to do – the work he was made to do – is only half a man. I tell you as surely as I'm standing here, that if you take Rupert Cargill away from his work and make it impossible for him to go on with that work, the day will come when you will have to stand by and see the man you love unhappy, unfulfilled – old before his time – tired and disheartened – only living with half his life. And if you think your love, or any woman's love, can make up to him for that, then I tell you plainly that you're a damned sentimental little fool.'

He stopped. He leaned back in his chair. He passed his hand through his hair.

Averil said, 'You say all this to me. But how do I know –' She broke off and began again, 'How do I know –'

'That it's true? I can only say that it's what I believe to be true and that *it is what I know of my own knowledge*. I'm speaking to you, Averil, as a man – as well as a father.'

'Yes,' said Averil. 'I see . . .'

Rodney said, and his voice was tired now and sounded muffled:

'It's up to you, Averil, to examine what I have told you, and to accept or reject it. I believe you have courage and clear-sightedness.'

Averil went slowly towards the door. She stopped with her hand on the handle and looked back.

Joan was startled by the sudden, bitter vindictiveness of her voice when she spoke.

'Don't imagine,' she said, 'that I shall ever be grateful to you, Father. I think – I think I hate you.'

And she went out and closed the door behind her.

Joan made a motion to go after her, but Rodney stopped her with a gesture.

'Leave her alone,' he said. 'Leave her alone. Don't you understand? We've won . . .'

Chapter Eight

And that, Joan reflected, had been the end of that.

Averil had gone about, very silent, answering in monosyllables when she was spoken to, never spoke if she could help it. She had got thinner and paler.

A month later she had expressed a wish to go to London and train in a secretarial school.

Rodney had assented at once. Averil had left them with no pretence of distress over the parting.

When she had come home on a visit three months later, she had been quite normal in manner and had seemed, from her account, to be having quite a gay life in London.

Joan was relieved and expressed her relief to Rodney.

'The whole thing has blown over completely. I never thought for a moment it was really serious – just one of those silly fancies girls get.'

Rodney looked at her, smiled, and said, 'Poor little Joan.'

That phrase of his always annoyed her.

'Well, you must admit it *was* worrying at the time.'

'Yes,' he said, 'it was certainly worrying. But it wasn't your worry, was it, Joan?'

'What do you mean? Anything that affects the children upsets me far more than it upsets them.'

'Does it?' Rodney said. 'I wonder . . .'

It was true, Joan thought, that there was now a certain coldness between Averil and her father. They had always been such friends. Now there seemed little except formal politeness between them. On the other hand, Averil had been quite charming, in her cool, noncommittal way, to her mother.

I expect, thought Joan, that she appreciates me better now that she doesn't live at home.

She herself certainly welcomed Averil's visits. Averil's cool, good sense seemed to ease things in the household.

Barbara was now grown up and was proving difficult.

Joan was increasingly distressed by her younger daughter's choice of friends. She seemed to have no kind of discrimination. There were plenty of nice girls in Crayminster, but Barbara, out of sheer perversity, it seemed, would have none of them.

'They're so hideously *dull*, Mother.'

'Nonsense, Barbara. I'm sure both Mary and Alison are charming girls, full of fun.'

'They're perfectly awful. They wear *snoods*.'

Joan had stared, bewildered.

'Really, Barbara – what do you mean? What can it matter?'

'It does. It's a kind of symbol.'

'I think you're talking nonsense, darling. There's Pamela Grayling – her mother used to be a great friend of mine. Why not go about with her a bit more?'

'Oh, Mother, she's hopelessly dreary, not amusing a bit.'

'Well, I think they're all very nice girls.'

'Yes, nice and deadly. And what does it matter what *you* think?'

'That's very rude, Barbara.'

'Well, what I mean is, you don't have to go about with them. So it's what *I* think matters. I like Betty Earle and Primrose Deane but you always stick your nose in the air when I bring them to tea.'

'Well, frankly, darling, they are rather dreadful – Betty's father runs those awful charabanc tours and simply hasn't got an *h*.'

'He's got lots of money, though.'

'Money isn't everything, Barbara.'

'The whole point is, Mother, can I choose my own friends, or can't I?'

'Of course you can, Barbara, but you must let yourself be guided by me. You are very young still.'

'That means I can't. It's pretty sickening the way I can't do a single thing I want to do! This place is an absolute prison house.'

And it was just then that Rodney had come in and had said, 'What's a prison house?'

Barbara cried out, 'Home is!'

And instead of taking the matter seriously Rodney had simply laughed and had said teasingly, 'Poor little Barbara – treated like a black slave.'

'Well, I am.'

'Quite right, too. I approve of slavery for daughters.'

And Barbara had hugged him and said breathlessly, 'Darling Dads, you are so – so – ridiculous. I never can be annoyed with you for long.'

Joan had begun indignantly, 'I should hope not –'

But Rodney was laughing, and when Barbara had gone out of the room, he had said, 'Don't take things too seriously, Joan. Young fillies have to kick up their heels a bit.'

'But these awful friends of hers –'

'A momentary phase of liking the flamboyant. It will pass. Don't worry, Joan.'

Very easy, Joan had thought indignantly, to say 'Don't worry.' What would happen to them all if she didn't worry? Rodney was far too easy going, and he couldn't possibly understand a mother's feelings.

Yet trying as Barbara's choice of girl friends had been, it was as nothing to the anxiety occasioned by the men she seemed to like.

George Harmon and that very objectionable young Wilmore – not only a member of the rival solicitor's firm (a firm that undertook the more dubious legal business of the town) but a young man who drank too much, talked too loudly, and was too fond of the race track. It was with young Wilmore that Barbara had disappeared from the Town Hall on the night of the Christmas Charity Dance, and had reappeared five dances later, sending a guilty but defiant glance towards where her mother was sitting.

They had been sitting out, it seemed, on the roof – a thing that only fast girls did, so Joan told Barbara, and it had distressed her very much.

'Don't be so Edwardian, Mother. It's absurd.'

'I'm not at all Edwardian. And let me tell you, Barbara, a lot of the old ideas about chaperonage are coming back into favour. Girls don't go about with young men as they did ten years ago.'

'Really, Mother, anyone would think I was going off week-ending with Tom Wilmore.'

'Don't talk like that, Barbara, I won't have it. And I heard you were seen in the Dog and Duck with George Harmon.'

'Oh, we were just doing a pub crawl.'

'Well, you're far too young to do anything of the kind. I don't like the way girls drink spirits nowadays.'

'I was only having beer. Actually we were playing darts.'

'Well, I don't like it, Barbara. And what's more I won't have it. I don't like George Harmon or Tom Wilmore and I won't have them in the house any more, do you understand?'

'O.K., Mother, it's your house.'

'Anyway I don't see what you like in them.'

Barbara shrugged her shoulders. 'Oh, I don't know. They're exciting.'

'Well, I won't have them asked to the house, do you hear?'

After that Joan had been annoyed when Rodney brought young Harmon home to Sunday supper one night. It was, she felt, so weak of Rodney. She herself put on her most glacial manner, and the young man seemed suitably abashed, in spite of the friendly way Rodney talked to him, and the pains he took to put him at his ease. George Harmon alternately talked too loud, or mumbled, boasted and then became apologetic.

Later that night, Joan took Rodney to task with some sharpness.

'Surely you must realize I'd told Barbara I wouldn't have him here?'

'I knew, Joan, but that's a mistake. Barbara has very little judgment. She takes people at their own valuation. She doesn't know the shoddy from the real. Seeing people against an alien background, she doesn't know where she is. That's why she needs to see people against her own background. She's been thinking of young Harmon as a dangerous and dashing figure, not just a foolish and boastful young man who drinks too much and has never done a proper day's work in his life.'

'*I* could have told her that!'

Rodney smiled.

'Oh, Joan, dear, nothing that you and I say is going to impress the younger generation.'

The truth of that was made plain to Joan when Averil came down on one of her brief visits.

This time it was Tom Wilmore who was being entertained. Against Averil's cool, critical distaste, Tom did not show to advantage.

Afterwards Joan caught a snatch of conversation between the sisters.

'You don't like him, Averil?'

And Averil, hunching disdainful shoulders had replied crisply, 'I think he's dreadful. Your taste in men, Barbara, is really too awful.'

Thereafter, Wilmore had disappeared from the scene, and the fickle Barbara had murmured one day, 'Tom Wilmore? Oh, but he's dreadful.' With complete and wide-eyed conviction.

Joan set herself to have tennis parties and ask people to the house, but Barbara refused stoutly to co-operate.

'Don't fuss so, Mother. You're always wanting to ask people. I hate having people, and you always will ask such terrible duds.'

Offended, Joan said sharply that she washed her hands of Barbara's amusement. 'I'm sure I don't know *what* you want!'

'I just want to be let alone.'

Barbara was really a most difficult child, Joan said sharply to Rodney. Rodney agreed, a little frown between his eyes.

'If she would only just say what she wants,' Joan continued.

'She doesn't know herself. She's very young, Joan.'

'That's just why she needs to have things decided for her.'

'No, my dear – she's got to find her own feet. Just let her be – let her bring her friends here if she wants to, but don't *organize* things. That's what seems to antagonize the young.'

So like a man, Joan thought with some exasperation. All for leaving things alone and being vague. Poor, dear Rodney, he always had been rather vague, now she came to think of it. It was she who had to be the practical one! And yet everyone said that he was such a shrewd lawyer.

Joan remembered an evening when Rodney had read from the local paper an announcement of George Harmon's marriage to Primrose Deane and had added with a teasing smile:

'An old flame of yours, eh, Babs?'

Barbara had laughed with considerable amusement.

'I know. I was awfully keen on him. He really is pretty dreadful, isn't he? I mean, he really *is*.'

'I always thought him a most unprepossessing young man. I couldn't imagine what you saw in him.'

'No more can I now.' Barbara at eighteen spoke detachedly of the follies of seventeen. 'But really, you know, Dads, I did think I was in love with him. I thought Mother would try to part us, and then I was going to run away with him, and if you or Mother stopped us, then I made up my mind I should put my head in the gas oven and kill myself.'

'Quite the Juliet touch!'

With a shade of disapproval, Barbara said, 'I meant it, Daddy. After all, if you can't bear a thing, you just *have* to kill yourself.'

And Joan, unable to bear keeping silent any longer, broke in sharply.

'Don't say such wicked things, Barbara. You don't know what you're talking about!'

'I forgot you were there, Mother. Of course, *you* wouldn't ever do a thing like that. *You'd* always be calm and sensible, whatever happened.'

'I should hope so indeed.'

Joan kept her temper with a little difficulty. She said to Rodney when Barbara had left the room:

'You shouldn't encourage the child in such nonsense.'

'Oh, she might as well talk it out of her system.'

'Of course, she'd never really do any of these dreadful things she talks about.'

Rodney was silent and Joan looked at him in surprise.

'Surely you don't think –'

'No, no, not really. Not when she's older, when she's got her balance. But Barbara is very unstable emotionally, Joan, we might as well face it.'

'It's all so ridiculous!'

'Yes, to us – who have a sense of proportion. But not to her. She's always in deadly earnest. She can't see beyond the mood of the moment. She has no detachment and no humour. Sexually, she is precocious –'

'Really, Rodney! You make things sound like – like one of those horrid cases in the police court.'

'Horrid cases in the police court concern living human beings, remember.'

'Yes, but nicely brought up girls like Barbara don't –'

'Don't what, Joan?'

'Must we talk like this?'

Rodney sighed.

'No. No, of course not. But I wish, yes, I really do wish that Barbara could meet some decent young fellow and fall properly in love with him.'

And after that it had really seemed like an answer to prayer, when young William Wray had come home from Iraq to stay with his aunt, Lady Herriot.

Joan had seen him first one day about a week after his arrival. He had been ushered into the drawing-room one afternoon when Barbara was out. Joan had looked up surprised from her writing table and had seen a tall, sturdily built young man with a jutting out chin, a very pink face, and a pair of steady blue eyes.

Blushing still pinker, Bill Wray had mumbled to his collar that he was Lady Herriot's nephew and that he had called – er – to return Miss Scudamore's racket which she had – er – left behind the other day.

Joan pulled her wits together and greeted him graciously.

Barbara was so careless, she said. Left her things all over the place. Barbara was out at the moment, but probably she would be back before long. Mr Wray must stay and have some tea.

Mr Wray was quite willing, it seemed, so Joan rang the bell for tea, and inquired after Mr Wray's aunt.

Lady Herriot's health occupied about five minutes, and then conversation began to halt a little. Mr Wray was not very helpful. He remained very pink in the face and sat very bolt upright and had a vague look of suffering some internal agony. Luckily tea came and made a diversion.

Joan was still prattling kindly, but with a slight sense of effort when Rodney, much to her relief, returned a little earlier than usual from the office. Rodney was very helpful. He talked of Iraq, drew the boy out with some simple questions, and presently some of Bill Wray's agonized stiffness began to relax. Soon he was talking almost easily. Presently Rodney took him off to his study. It was nearly seven o'clock when Bill, still it seemed reluctantly, took his departure.

'Nice lad,' said Rodney.

'Yes, quite. Rather shy.'

'Decidedly.' Rodney seemed amused. 'But I don't think he's usually quite so diffident.'

'What a frightfully long time he stayed!'

'Over two hours.'

'You must be terribly tired, Rodney.'

'Oh no, I enjoyed it. He's got a very good headpiece, that boy, and rather an unusual outlook on things. The philosophic bent of mind. He's got character as well as brains. Yes, I liked him.'

'He must have liked you – to stay talking as long as he did.'

Rodney's look of amusement returned.

'Oh, he wasn't staying to talk to me. He was hoping for Barbara's return. Come, Joan, don't you know love when you see it? The poor fellow was stiff with embarrassment. That's why he was as red as a beetroot. It must have taken a great effort for him to nerve himself to come here – and when he did, no glimpse of his lady. Yes, one of those cases of love at first sight.'

Presently when Barbara came hurrying into the house, just in time for dinner, Joan said:

'One of your young men has been here, Barbara, Lady Herriot's nephew. He brought back your racket.'

'Oh, Bill Wray? So he did find it? It seemed to have disappeared completely the other evening.'

'He was here some time,' said Joan.

'Pity I missed him. I went to the pictures with the Crabbes. A frightfully stupid film. Did you get awfully bored with Bill?'

'No,' said Rodney. 'I liked him. We talked Near Eastern politics. You'd have been bored, I expect.'

'I like to hear about queer parts of the world. I'd love to travel. I get so fed up always staying in Crayminster. At any rate, Bill is different.'

'You can always train for a job,' suggested Rodney.

'Oh, a job!' Barbara wrinkled up her nose. 'You know, Dads, I'm an idle devil. I don't like work.'

'No more do most people, I suspect,' said Rodney.

Barbara rushed at him and hugged him.

'You work much too hard. I've always thought so. It's a shame!'

Then, releasing her hold, she said, 'I'll give Bill a ring. He said something about going to the point to point over at Marsden . . .'

Rodney stood looking after her as she walked away towards the telephone at the back of the hall. It was an odd look, questioning, uncertain.

He had liked Bill Wray, yes, undoubtedly he had liked Bill from the first. Why, then, had he looked so worried, so harassed, when Barbara had burst in and announced that she and Bill were engaged and they meant to be married at once so that she could go back to Baghdad with him?

Bill was young, well connected, with money of his own, and good prospects. Why then, did Rodney demur, and suggest a longer engagement? Why did he go about frowning, looking uncertain and perplexed?

And then, just before the marriage, that sudden outburst, that insistence that Barbara was too young?

Oh well, Barbara had soon settled that objection, and six months after she had married her Bill and departed for Baghdad, Averil in her turn had announced her engagement to a stockbroker, a man called Edward Harrison-Wilmott.

He was a quiet, pleasant man of about thirty-four and extremely well off.

So really, Joan thought, everything seemed to be turning out splendidly. Rodney was rather quiet about Averil's engagement, but when she pressed him he said, 'Yes, yes, it's the best thing. He's a nice fellow.'

After Averil's marriage, Joan and Rodney were alone in the house.

Tony, after training at an agricultural college and then failing to pass his exams, and altogether causing them a good deal of anxiety, had finally gone out to South Africa where a client of Rodney's had a big orange farm in Rhodesia.

Tony wrote them enthusiastic letters, though not very lengthy ones. Then he had written and announced his engagement to a girl from Durban. Joan was rather upset at the idea of her son marrying a girl they had never even seen. She had no money, either – and really, as she said to Rodney, what did they know about her? Nothing at all.

Rodney said that it was Tony's funeral, and that they must hope for the best. She looked a nice girl, he thought, from the photographs Tony had sent, and she seemed willing to begin with Tony in a small way up in Rhodesia.

'And I suppose they'll spend their entire lives out there and hardly ever come home. Tony ought to have been forced to go into the firm – I said so at the time!'

Rodney had smiled and said that he wasn't very good at forcing people to do things.

'No, but really, Rodney, you ought to have *insisted*. He would soon have settled down. People do.'

Yes, Rodney said, that was true. But it was, he thought, too great a risk.

Risk? Joan said she didn't understand. What did he mean by risk?

Rodney said he meant the risk that the boy mightn't be happy.

Joan said she sometimes lost patience with all this talk of happiness. Nobody seemed to think of anything else. Happiness wasn't the only thing in life. There were other things much more important.

Such as, Rodney had asked?

Well, Joan said – after a moment's hesitation – duty, for instance.

Rodney said that surely it could never be a duty to become a solicitor.

Slightly annoyed, Joan replied that he knew perfectly what she meant. It was Tony's duty to please his father and not disappoint him.

'Tony hasn't disappointed me.'

But surely, Joan exclaimed, Rodney didn't like his only son being far away half across the world, living where they could never see the boy.

'No,' said Rodney with a sigh. 'I must admit that I miss Tony very much. He was such a sunny, cheerful creature to have about the house. Yes, I miss him . . .'

'That's what I say. You should have been firm!'

'After all, Joan, it's Tony's life. Not ours. Ours is over and done with, for better or worse – the active part of it, I mean.'

'Yes – well – I suppose that's so in a way.'

She thought a minute and then she said, 'Well, it's been a very nice life. And still is, of course.'

'I'm glad of that.'

He was smiling at her. Rodney had a nice smile, a teasing smile. Sometimes he looked as though he was smiling at something that you yourself didn't see.

'The truth is,' said Joan, 'that you and I are really very well suited to each other.'

'Yes, we haven't had many quarrels.'

'And then we've been lucky with our children. It would have been terrible if they'd turned out badly or been unhappy or something like that.'

'Funny Joan,' Rodney had said.

'Well but, Rodney, it really *would* have been very upsetting.'

'I don't think anything would upset you for long, Joan.'

'Well,' she considered the point. 'Of course I have got a very equable temperament. I think it's one's duty, you know, not to give way to things.'

'An admirable and convenient sentiment!'

'It's nice, isn't it,' said Joan smiling, 'to feel one's made a success of things?'

'Yes.' Rodney had sighed. 'Yes, it must be very nice.'

Joan laughed and putting her hand on his arm, gave it a little shake.

'Don't be modest, Rodney. No solicitor has got a bigger practice round here than you have. It's far bigger than in Uncle Henry's time.'

'Yes, the firm is doing well.'

'And there's more capital coming in with the new partner. Do you mind having a new partner?'

Rodney shook his head.

'Oh no, we need young blood. Both Alderman and I are getting on.'

Yes, she thought, it was true. There was a lot of grey in Rodney's dark hair.

* * *

Joan roused herself, and glanced at her watch.

The morning was passing quite quickly, and there had been no recurrence of those distressing chaotic thoughts which seemed to force themselves into her mind so inopportunely.

Well, that showed, didn't it, that 'discipline' was the watchword needed. To arrange one's thoughts in an orderly manner, recalling only those memories that were pleasant and satisfactory. That is what she had done this morning – and see how quickly the morning had passed. In about an hour and a half it would be lunch time. Perhaps she had better go out for a short stroll, keeping quite near the rest house. That would just make a little change before coming in to eat another of those hot, heavy meals.

She went into the bedroom, put on her double felt hat and went out.

The Arab boy was kneeling on the ground, his face turned towards Mecca, and was bending forward and straightening himself, uttering words in a high nasal chant.

The Indian, coming up unseen, said instructively just behind Joan's shoulder, 'Him make midday prayer.'

Joan nodded. The information, she felt, was unnecessary. She could see perfectly well what the boy was doing.

'Him say Allah very compassionate, Allah very merciful.'

'I know,' said Joan and moved away, strolling gently towards the barbed wire conglomeration that marked the railway station.

She remembered having seen six or seven Arabs trying to move a dilapidated Ford that had stuck in the sand, all pulling and tugging in opposite directions, and how her son-in-law, William, had explained to her that in addition to these well meant but abortive efforts, they were saying hopefully, 'Allah is very merciful.'

Allah, she thought, had need to be, since it was certain that nothing but a miracle would extract the car if they all continued to tug in opposite directions.

The curious thing was that they all seemed quite happy about it and enjoying themselves. Inshallah, they would say, if God wills, and would thereupon bend no intelligent endeavour on the satisfaction of their desires. It was not a way of living that commended itself to Joan. One should take thought and make plans for the morrow. Though perhaps if one lived in the middle of nowhere like Tell Abu Hamid it might not be so necessary.

If one were here for long, reflected Joan, one would forget even what day of the week it was . . .

And she thought, Let me see, today is Thursday . . . yes, Thursday, I got here on Monday night.

She had arrived now at the tangle of barbed wire and she saw, a little way beyond it, a man in some kind of uniform with a rifle. He was leaning up against a large case and she supposed he was guarding the station or the frontier.

He seemed to be asleep and Joan thought she had better not go any farther in case he might wake up and shoot her. It was the sort of thing, she felt, that would not be at all impossible at Tell Abu Hamid.

She retraced her steps, making a slight detour so as to encircle the rest house. In that way she would eke out the time and run no risk of that strange feeling of agoraphobia (if it had been agoraphobia).

Certainly, she thought with approval, the morning had gone very successfully. She had gone over in her mind the things for which she had to be thankful. Averil's marriage to dear Edward, such a solid, dependable sort of man – and so well off, too; Averil's house in London was quite delightful – so handy for Harrods. And Barbara's marriage. And Tony's – though that really wasn't quite so satisfactory – in fact they knew nothing about it – and

Tony himself was not as entirely satisfactory as a son should be. Tony should have remained in Crayminster and gone into Alderman, Scudamore and Witney's. He should have married a nice English girl, fond of outdoor life, and followed in his father's footsteps.

Poor Rodney, with his dark hair streaked with grey, and no son to succeed him at the office.

The truth was that Rodney had been much too weak with Tony. He should have put his foot down. Firmness, that was the thing. Why, thought Joan, where would Rodney be, I should like to know, if I hadn't put *my* foot down? She felt a warm little glow of self approval. Crippled with debts, probably, and trying to raise a mortgage like Farmer Hoddesdon. She wondered if Rodney really quite appreciated what she had done for him . . .

Joan stared ahead of her at the swimming line of the horizon. A queer watery effect. Of course, she thought, mirage!

Yes, that was it, mirage . . . just like pools of water in the sand. Not at all what one thought of as mirage – she had always imagined trees and cities – something much more concrete.

But even this unspectacular watery effect was queer – it made one feel – what *was* reality?

Mirage, she thought, mirage. The word seemed important.

What had she been thinking of? Oh, of course, Tony, and how exceedingly selfish and thoughtless he had been.

It had always been extremely difficult to get at Tony. He was so vague, so apparently acquiescent, and yet in his quiet, amiable, smiling way, he did exactly as he liked. Tony had never been quite so devoted to her as she felt a son ought to be to his mother. In fact he really seemed to care for his father most.

She remembered how Tony, as a small boy of seven,

in the middle of the night, had entered the dressing-room where Rodney was sleeping, and had announced quietly and unromantically:

'I think, Father, I must have eaten a toadstool instead of a mushroom, because I have a very bad pain and I think I am going to die. So I have come here to die with you.'

Actually, it had been nothing to do with toadstools or mushrooms. It had been acute appendicitis and the boy had been operated on within twenty-four hours. But it still seemed to Joan queer that the child should have gone to Rodney and not to her. Far more natural for Tony to have come to his mother.

Yes, Tony had been trying in many ways. Lazy at school. Slack over games. And though he was a very good-looking boy and the kind of boy she was proud to take about with her, he never seemed to want to be taken about, and had an irritating habit of melting into the landscape just when she was looking for him.

'Protective colouring,' Averil had called it, Joan remembered. 'Tony is much cleverer at protective colouring than we are,' she had said.

Joan had not quite understood her meaning, but she had felt vaguely a little hurt by it . . .

Joan looked at her watch. No need to get too hot walking. Back to the rest house now. It had been an excellent morning – no incidents of any kind – no unpleasant thoughts, no sensations of agoraphobia –

Really, some inner voice in her exclaimed, you are talking just like a hospital nurse. What do you think you are, Joan Scudamore? an invalid? a mental case? And why do you feel so proud of yourself and yet so tired? Is there anything extraordinary in having passed a pleasant, normal morning?

She went quickly into the rest house, and was delighted

to see that there were tinned pears for lunch as a change.

After lunch she went and lay down on her bed.

If she could sleep until tea time . . .

But she did not feel even inclined to sleep. Her brain felt bright and wakeful. She lay there with closed eyes, but her body felt alert and tense, as though it were waiting for something . . . as though it were watchful, ready to defend itself against some lurking danger. All her muscles were taut.

I must relax, Joan thought, I must relax.

But she couldn't relax. Her body was stiff and braced. Her heart was beating a little faster than was normal. Her mind was alert and suspicious.

The whole thing reminded her of something. She searched and at last the right comparison came to her – a dentist's waiting-room.

The feeling of something definitely unpleasant just ahead of you, the determination to reassure yourself, to put off thinking of it, and the knowledge that each minute was bringing the ordeal nearer . . .

But what ordeal – what was she expecting?

What was going to happen?

The lizards, she thought, have all gone back into their holes . . . that's because there's a storm coming . . . the quiet – before a storm . . . waiting . . . waiting . . .

Good Heavens, she was getting quite incoherent again.

Miss Gilbey . . . discipline . . . a Spiritual Retreat . . .

A Retreat! She must meditate. There was something about repeating Om . . . Theosophy? Or Buddhism . . .

No, no, stick to her own religion. Meditate on God. On the love of God. *God*. . . Our Father, which art in Heaven . . .

Her own father – his squarely trimmed naval brown beard, his deep piercing blue eyes, his liking for everything to be trim and shipshape in the house. A kindly martinet, that was her father, a typical retired Admiral. And her mother, tall, thin, vague, untidy, with a careless sweetness that made people, even when she most exasperated them, find all kinds of excuses for her.

Her mother going out to parties with odd gloves and a crooked skirt and a hat pinned askew to a bun of iron grey hair, and happily and serenely unconscious of anything amiss about her appearance. And the anger of the Admiral – always directed on his daughters, never on his wife.

'Why can't you girls look after your mother? What do you mean by letting her go out like that! I will *not* have such slackness!' he would roar. And the three girls would say submissively:

'No, Father.' And afterwards, to each other, 'It's all very well, but really Mother is impossible!'

Joan had been very fond of her mother, of course, but her fondness had not blinded her to the fact that her mother was really a very tiresome woman – her complete lack of method and consistency hardly atoned for by her gay irresponsibility and warm-hearted impulsiveness.

It had come as quite a shock to Joan, clearing up her mother's papers after her mother's death, to come across a letter from her father, written on the twentieth anniversary of their marriage.

> I grieve deeply that I cannot be with you today, dear heart. I would like to tell you in this letter all that your love has meant to me all these years and how you are more dear to me today than you have ever been before. Your love has been the crowning blessing of my life and I thank God for it and for you . . .

Somehow she had never realized that her father felt quite like that about her mother . . .

Joan thought, Rodney and I will have been married twenty-five years this December. Our silver wedding.

How nice, she thought, if he were to write such a letter to me . . .

She concocted a letter in her mind.

> Dearest Joan – I feel I must write down all I owe to you – and what you have meant to me – You have no idea, I am sure, how your love has been the crowning blessing . . .

Somehow, Joan thought, breaking off this imaginative exercise, it didn't seem very real. Impossible to imagine Rodney writing such a letter . . . much as he loved her . . . much as he loved her . . .

Why repeat that so defiantly? Why feel such a queer, cold little shiver? What had she been thinking about before that?

Of course! Joan came to herself with a shock. She was supposed to be engaged in spiritual meditation. Instead of that she had been thinking of mundane matters – of her father and mother, dead these many years.

Dead, leaving her alone.

Alone in the desert. Alone in this very unpleasant prison-like room.

With nothing to think about but herself.

She sprang up. No use lying here when one couldn't go to sleep.

She hated these high rooms with their small gauze-covered windows. They hemmed you in. They made you feel small, insect-like. She wanted a big, airy drawing-room, with nice cheerful cretonnes and a crackling fire in the grate and people – lots of people – people you could go and see and people who would come and see you . . .

Oh, the train *must* come soon – it had got to come soon. Or a car – or *something* . . .

'I can't stay here,' said Joan aloud. 'I can't stay here!'

(Talking to yourself, she thought, that's a very bad sign.)

She had some tea and then she went out. She didn't feel she could sit still and think.

She would go out and walk, and she wouldn't think.

Thinking, that was what upset you. Look at these people who lived in this place – the Indian, the Arab boy, the cook. She felt quite sure they never thought.

Sometimes I sits and thinks, and sometimes I just sits . . .

Who had said that? What an admirable way of life!

She wouldn't think, she would just walk. Not too far away from the rest house just in case – well, just in case . . .

Describe a large circle. Round and round. Like an animal. Humiliating. Yes, humiliating but there it was. She had got to be very, very careful of herself. Otherwise –

Otherwise what? She didn't know. She hadn't any idea.

She mustn't think of Rodney, she mustn't think of Averil, she mustn't think of Tony, she mustn't think of Barbara. She mustn't think of Blanche Haggard. She mustn't think of scarlet rhododendron buds. (Particularly she mustn't think of scarlet rhododendron buds!) She mustn't think of poetry . . .

She mustn't think of Joan Scudamore. But that's myself! No, it isn't. Yes, it is . . .

If you had nothing but yourself to think about what would you find out about yourself?

'I don't want to know,' said Joan aloud.

The sound of her voice astonished her. What was it that she didn't want to know?

A battle, she thought, I'm fighting a losing battle.

But against whom? Against what?

Never mind, she thought. I don't want to know –

Hang on to that. It was a good phrase.

Odd the feeling that there was someone walking with her. Someone she knew quite well. If she turned her head

. . . well, she had turned her head but there was no one. No one at all.

Yet the feeling that there was someone persisted. It frightened her. Rodney, Averil, Tony, Barbara, none of them would help her, none of them could help her, none of them wanted to help her. None of them cared.

She would go back to the rest house and get away from whoever it was who was spying on her.

The Indian was standing outside the wire door. Joan was swaying a little as she walked. The way he stared annoyed her.

'What is it?' she said. 'What's the matter?'

'Memsahib not look well. Perhaps Memsahib have fever?'

That was it. Of course, that was it. She had fever! How stupid not to have thought of that before.

She hurried in. She must take her temperature, look for her quinine. She had got some quinine with her somewhere.

She got out her thermometer and put it under her tongue.

Fever – of course it was fever! The incoherence – the nameless dreads – the apprehension – the fast beating of her heart.

Purely physical, the whole thing.

She took out the thermometer and looked at it.

98.2. If anything she was a shade below normal.

She got through the evening somehow. She was by now really alarmed about herself. It wasn't sun – it wasn't fever – it must be nerves.

'Just nerves,' people said. She had said so herself about other people. Well, she hadn't known. She knew now. Just nerves, indeed! Nerves were hell! What she needed was a doctor, a nice, sympathetic doctor, and a nursing home and a kindly, efficient nurse who would never leave the room. 'Mrs Scudamore must never be left alone.' What she had got was a white-washed prison in the middle of a desert, a semi-intelligent Indian, a completely imbecile Arab boy, and a cook who would presently send in a meal of rice and tinned salmon and baked beans and hard-boiled eggs.

All wrong, thought Joan, completely the wrong treatment for my sort of case . . .

After dinner she went to her room and looked at her aspirin bottle. There were six tablets left. Recklessly she took them all. It was leaving her nothing for tomorrow, but she felt she must try something. Never again, she thought, will I go travelling without some proper sleeping stuff with me.

She undressed and lay down apprehensively.

Strangely enough she fell asleep almost immediately.

That night she dreamed that she was in a big prison building with winding corridors. She was trying to get out but she couldn't find the way, and yet, all the time, she knew quite well that she *did* know it . . .

You've only got to remember, she kept saying to herself earnestly, you've only got to remember.

In the morning she woke up feeling quite peaceful, though tired.

'You've only got to remember,' she said to herself.

She got up and dressed and had breakfast.

She felt quite all right, just a little apprehensive, that was all.

I suppose it will all start again soon, she thought to herself. Oh well, there's nothing I can do about it.

She sat inertly in a chair. Presently she would go out, but not just yet.

She wouldn't try to think about anything in particular – and she wouldn't try not to think. Both were much too tiring. She would just let herself drift.

The outer office of Alderman, Scudamore and Witney – the deed boxes labelled in white. Estate of Sir Jasper Ffoulkes, deceased. Colonel Etchingham Williams. Just like stage properties.

Peter Sherston's face looking up bright and eager from his desk. How very like his mother he was – no, not quite – he had Charles Sherston's eyes. That quick, shifty, sideways look. I wouldn't trust him too far if I were Rodney, she had thought.

Funny that she should have thought that!

After Leslie Sherston's death, Sherston had gone completely to pieces. He had drunk himself to death in record time. The children had been salvaged by relations. The third child, a little girl, had died six months after its birth.

John, the eldest boy, had gone into woods and forests. He was somewhere out in Burma now. Joan remembered Leslie and her handprinted linen covers. If John was like his mother, and had her desire to see things that grew fast, he must be very happy now. She had heard that he was doing very well.

Peter Sherston had come to Rodney and had expressed his desire to be taken into the office.

'My mother told me she was sure you would help me, sir.'

An attractive, forthright boy, smiling, eager, always anxious to please – the more attractive, Joan had always thought, of the two.

Rodney had been glad to take the boy. It had made up to him a little, perhaps, for the fact that his own son had preferred to go overseas and had cut himself off from his family.

In time, perhaps, Rodney might have come to look upon Peter almost as a son. He was often at the house and was always charming to Joan. Easy, attractive manners – not quite so unctuous as his father's had been.

And then one day Rodney had come home looking

worried and ill. In response to her questions he had replied impatiently that it was nothing, nothing at all. But about a week later he mentioned that Peter was leaving – had decided to go to an aircraft factory.

'Oh, Rodney, and you've been so good to him. And we both liked him so much!'

'Yes – an attractive lad.'

'What was the trouble? Was he lazy?'

'Oh no, he's a good head for figures and all that sort of thing.'

'Like his father?'

'Yes, like his father. But all these lads are attracted to the new discoveries – flying – that kind of thing.'

But Joan was not listening. Her own words had suggested to her a certain train of thought. Peter Sherston had left very suddenly.

'Rodney – there wasn't anything *wrong*, was there?'

'Wrong? What do you mean?'

'I mean – well, like his father. His mouth is like Leslie's – but he's got that funny, shifty look in the eyes that his father always had. Oh, Rodney, it's true, isn't it? He *did* do something?'

Rodney said slowly, 'There was just a little trouble.'

'Over the accounts? He took money?'

'I'd rather not talk about it, Joan. It was nothing important.'

'Crooked like his father! Isn't heredity queer?'

'Very queer. It seems to work the wrong way.'

'You mean he might just as well have taken after Leslie? Still, she wasn't a particularly efficient person, was she?'

Rodney said in a dry voice, 'I'm of the opinion that she was very efficient. She stuck to her job and did it well.'

'Poor thing.'

Rodney said irritably, 'I wish you wouldn't always pity her. It annoys me.'

'But, Rodney, how unkind of you. She really had an awfully sad life.'

'I never think of her that way.'

'And then her death –'

'I'd rather you didn't talk about that.'

He turned away.

Everybody, thought Joan, was afraid of cancer. They flinched away from the word. They called it, if possible, something else – a malignant growth – a serious operation – an incurable complaint – something internal. Even Rodney didn't like the mention of it. Because, after all, one never knew – one in every twelve, wasn't it, died of it? And it often seemed to attack the healthiest people. People who had never had anything else the matter with them.

Joan remembered the day that she heard the news from Mrs Lambert in the Market Square.

'My dear, have you heard? Poor Mrs Sherston!'

'What about her?'

'Dead!' With gusto. And then the lowered voice. 'Internal, I believe . . . Impossible to operate . . . She suffered terrible pain, I hear. But very plucky. Kept on working until only a couple of weeks before the end – when they really *had* to keep her under morphia. My nephew's wife saw her only six weeks ago. She looked terribly ill and was as thin as a rail, but she was just the same, laughing and joking. I suppose people just can't believe they can never get well. Oh well, she had a sad life, poor woman. I daresay it's a merciful release . . .'

Joan had hurried home to tell Rodney, and Rodney had said quietly, Yes, he knew. He was the executor of her will, he said, and so they had communicated with him at once.

Leslie Sherston had not had very much to leave. What there was was to be divided between her children. The clause that did excite Crayminster was the direction that her body should be brought to Crayminster for burial. 'Because,' so ran the will, 'I was very happy there.'

So Leslie Adeline Sherston was laid to rest in the churchyard of St Mary's, Crayminster.

An odd request, some people thought, considering that it was in Crayminster that her husband had been convicted of fraudulent appropriation of bank funds. But other people said that it was quite natural. She had had a happy time there before all the trouble, and it was only natural that she should look back on it as a kind of lost Garden of Eden.

Poor Leslie – a tragic family altogether, for young Peter, after training as a test pilot, had crashed and been killed.

Rodney had been terribly cut up about it. In a queer way he seemed to blame himself for Peter's death.

'But really, Rodney, I don't see how you make that out. It was nothing to do with you.'

'Leslie sent him to me – she told him that I would give him a job and look after him.'

'Well, so you did. You took him into the office.'

'I know.'

'And he went wrong, and you didn't prosecute him or anything – you made up the deficit yourself, didn't you?'

'Yes, yes – it isn't that. Don't you see, that's *why* Leslie sent him to me, because she realized that he was weak, that he had Sherston's untrustworthiness. John was all right. She trusted me to look after Peter, to guard the weak spot. He was a queer mixture. He had Charles Sherston's crookedness and Leslie's courage. Armadales wrote me that he was the best pilot they'd had – absolutely fearless and a wizard – that's how they phrased it – with planes. The boy volunteered, you know, to try out a new secret device on a plane. It was known to be dangerous. That's how he was killed.'

'Well, I call that very creditable, very creditable indeed.'

Rodney gave a short dry laugh.

'Oh yes, Joan. But would you say that so complacently if it was your own son who had been killed like that? Would you be satisfied for Tony to have a creditable death?'

Joan stared.

'But Peter wasn't our son. It's entirely different.'

'I'm thinking of Leslie ... of what she would have felt ...'

Sitting in the rest house, Joan shifted a little in her chair.

Why had the Sherstons been so constantly in her thoughts ever since she had been here? She had other friends, friends who meant much more to her than any of the Sherstons had ever done.

She had never liked Leslie so very much, only felt sorry for her. Poor Leslie under her marble slab.

Joan shivered. I'm cold, she thought. I'm cold. Somebody is walking over my grave.

But it was Leslie Sherston's grave she was thinking about.

It's cold in here, she thought, cold and gloomy. I'll go out in the sunlight. I don't want to stay here any longer.

The churchyard – and Leslie Sherston's grave. And the scarlet, heavy rhododendron bud that fell from Rodney's coat.

Rough winds do shake the darling buds of May ...

Chapter Nine

Joan came out into the sunlight at almost a run.

She started walking quickly, hardly glancing at the dump of tins and the hens.

That was better. Warm sunlight.

Warm – not cold any longer.

She had got away from it all . . .

But what did she mean by 'got away from it all'?

The wraith of Miss Gilbey seemed suddenly to be close beside her, saying in impressive tones:

'Discipline your thoughts, Joan. Be more precise in your terms. Make up your mind exactly what it is from which you are running away.'

But she didn't know. She hadn't the least idea.

Some fear, some menacing and pursuing dread.

Something that had been always there – waiting – and all she could do was to dodge and twist and turn . . .

Really, Joan Scudamore, she said to herself, you are behaving in a very peculiar manner . . .

But saying so didn't help matters. There must be something badly wrong with her. It couldn't exactly be agoraphobia – (had she got that name right, or not? It worried her not to be sure) because this time she was anxious to escape from those cold, confining walls – to get out from them into space and sunlight. She felt better now that she was outside.

Go out! Go out into the sunshine! Get away from these thoughts.

She'd been here long enough. In this high-ceilinged room that was like a mausoleum.

Leslie Sherston's grave, and Rodney . . .

Leslie . . . Rodney . . .

Get out . . .

The sunshine . . .

So cold – in this room . . .

Cold, and alone . . .

She increased her pace. Get away from that dreadful mausoleum of a rest house. So grim, so hemmed in . . .

The sort of place where you could easily imagine ghosts.

What a stupid idea – it was practically a brand new building, only put up two years ago.

There couldn't be ghosts in a new building, everybody knew that.

No, if there were ghosts in the rest house, then she, Joan Scudamore, must have brought them with her.

Now that was a *very* unpleasant thought . . .

She quickened her pace.

At any rate, she thought determinedly, there's nobody with me now. I'm quite alone. There's not even anybody I could meet.

Like – who was it – Stanley and Livingstone? Meeting in the wilds of Africa.

Dr Livingstone, I presume.

Nothing like that here. Only one person she could meet here and that was Joan Scudamore.

What a comic idea! '*Meet Joan Scudamore.*' '*Pleased to meet you, Mrs Scudamore.*'

Really – quite an interesting idea . . .

Meet yourself . . .

Meet yourself . . .

Oh, God, she was frightened . . .

She was horribly frightened . . .

Her steps quickened into a run. She ran forward, stumbling a little. Her thoughts stumbled just like her feet did.

. . . I'm frightened . . .

. . . Oh, God, I'm so frightened . . .

. . . If only there was someone here. Someone to be with me . . .

Blanche, she thought. I wish Blanche were here.

Yes, Blanche was just the person she wanted . . .

Nobody near and dear to her. None of her friends.

Just Blanche . . .

Blanche, with her easy, warm-hearted kindness. Blanche was kind. You couldn't surprise Blanche or shock her.

And anyway, Blanche thought she was nice. Blanche thought she had made a success of life. Blanche was fond of her.

Nobody else was . . .

That was it – that was the thought that had been with her all along – that was what the real Joan Scudamore knew – had always known . . .

Lizards popping out of holes . . .

Truth . . .

Little bits of truth, popping out like lizards, saying, 'Here am I. You know me. You know me quite well. Don't pretend you don't.'

And she did know them – that was the awful part of it.

She could recognize each one of them.

Grinning at her, laughing at her.

All the little bits and pieces of truth. They'd been showing themselves to her ever since she'd arrived here. All she needed to do was to piece them together.

The whole story of her life – the real story of Joan Scudamore . . .

It was here waiting for her . . .

She had never needed to think about it before. It had been quite easy to fill her life with unimportant trivialities that left her no time for self-knowledge.

What was it Blanche had said?

'If you'd nothing to think about but yourself for days on end I wonder what you'd find out about yourself?'

And how superior, how smug, how stupid had been her answer:

'Would one find out anything one didn't know before?'

Sometimes, Mother, I don't think you know anything about anybody . . .

That had been Tony.

How right Tony had been.

She hadn't known anything about her children, anything about Rodney. She had loved them but she hadn't known.

She should have known.

If you loved people you should know about them.

You didn't know because it was so much easier to believe the pleasant, easy things that you would like to be true, and not distress yourself with the things that really were true.

Like Averil – Averil and the pain that Averil had suffered.

She hadn't wanted to recognize that Averil had suffered . . .

Averil who had always despised her . . .

Averil who had seen through her at a very early age . . .

Averil who had been broken and hurt by life and who, even now perhaps, was still a maimed creature.

But a creature with courage . . .

That was what she, Joan, had lacked. Courage.

'*Courage isn't everything*,' she had said.

And Rodney had said, '*Isn't it?* . . .'

Rodney had been right . . .

Tony, Averil, Rodney – all of them her accusers.

And Barbara?

What had been wrong with Barbara? Why had the doctor been so reticent? What was it they had all been hiding from her?

What had the child done – that passionate undisciplined child, who had married the first man who asked her so as to get away from home.

Yes, it was quite true – that was exactly what Barbara had done. She'd been unhappy at home. And she'd been unhappy because Joan hadn't taken the least trouble to make home happy for her.

She'd had no love for Barbara, no kind of understanding. Cheerfully and selfishly she had determined what was good for Barbara without the least regard for Barbara's tastes or wishes. She had had no welcome for Barbara's friends, had gently discouraged them. No wonder the idea of Baghdad had seemed to Barbara like a vista of escape.

She had married Bill Wray hastily and impulsively, and without (so Rodney said) loving him. And then what had happened?

A love affair? An unhappy love affair? That Major Reid, probably. Yes, that would explain the embarrassment when Joan had mentioned his name. Just the kind of man, she thought, to fascinate a silly child who wasn't yet properly grown up.

And then, in desperation, in one of those violent paroxysms of despair to which she had been prone from early childhood, those cataclysms when she lost all sense of proportion, she had tried – yes, that must be it – to take her own life.

And she had been very, very ill – dangerously ill.

Had Rodney known, Joan wondered? He had certainly tried to dissuade her from rushing out to Baghdad.

No, surely Rodney couldn't have known. He would have told her. Well, no, perhaps he wouldn't have told her. He certainly had done his best to stop her going.

But she had been absolutely determined. She had felt, she said, that she simply couldn't endure not to go out to the poor child.

Surely *that* had been a creditable impulse.

Only – wasn't even that a part, only, of the truth?

Hadn't she been attracted by the idea of the journey – the novelty – seeing a new part of the world? Hadn't she enjoyed the idea of playing the part of the devoted mother? Hadn't she seen herself as a charming, impulsive woman being welcomed by her ill daughter and her distracted son-in-law? How good of you, they would say, to come rushing out like that.

Really, of course, they hadn't been at all pleased to see her! They had been, quite frankly, dismayed. They had warned the doctor, guarded their tongues, done everything imaginable to prevent her from learning the truth. They didn't want her to know because they didn't trust her. Barbara hadn't trusted her. Keep it from Mother – that had probably been her one idea.

How relieved they had been when she had announced that she must go back. They had hidden it quite well, making polite protestations, suggesting that she might stay on for a while. But when she had just for a moment actually thought of doing so, how quick William had been to discourage her.

In fact, the only possible good that she had done by her hurried rush eastwards was the somewhat curious one of drawing Barbara and William together in their united effort to get rid of her and keep their secret. Odd if, after all, some positive good might come from her visit. Often, Joan remembered, Barbara, still weak, had looked appealingly at William, and William, responding, had hurried into speech, had explained some doubtful point, had fended off one of Joan's tactless questions.

And Barbara had looked at him gratefully – affectionately.

They had stood there on the platform, seeing her off. And Joan remembered how William had held Barbara's hand, and Barbara had leaned a little towards him.

'Courage, darling,' that was what he had been meaning. 'It's nearly over – she's going . . .'

And after the train had gone, they would go back to their bungalow at Alwyah and play with Mopsy – for they both loved Mopsy, that adorable baby who was such a ridiculous caricature of William – and Barbara would stay, 'Thank goodness she's gone and we've got the house to ourselves.'

Poor William, who loved Barbara so much and who must have been so unhappy, and yet who had never faltered in his love and tenderness.

'Don't worry about her!' Blanche had said. 'She'll be all right. There's the kid and everything.'

Kind Blanche, reassuring an anxiety that simply hadn't existed.

All she, Joan, had had in her mind was a superior disdainful pity for her old friend.

I thank thee, Lord, that I am not as this woman.

Yes, she had even dared to pray . . .

And now, at this moment, she would have given anything to have had Blanche with her!

Blanche, with her kindly, easy charity – her complete lack of condemnation of any living creature.

She had prayed that night at the railway rest house wrapped in that spurious mantle of superiority.

Could she pray now, when it seemed to her that she had no longer a rag to cover her?

Joan stumbled forward and fell on her knees.

. . . *God*, she prayed, *help me* . . .

. . . *I'm going mad, God* . . .

. . . *Don't let me go mad* . . .

. . . *Don't let me go on thinking* . . .

Silence . . .

Silence and sunlight . . .

And the pounding of her own heart . . .

God, she thought, *has forsaken me* . . .

... God won't help me ...

... I am alone – quite alone ...

That terrible silence ... that awful loneliness ...

Little Joan Scudamore ... silly, futile, pretentious little Joan Scudamore ...

All alone in the desert.

Christ, she thought, *was alone in the desert.*

For forty days and forty nights ...

... No, no, nobody could do that – nobody could bear it ...

The silence, the sun, the loneliness ...

Fear came upon her again – the fear of the vast empty spaces where man is alone except for God ...

She stumbled to her feet.

She must get back to the rest house – back to the rest house.

The Indian – the Arab boy – the hens – the empty tins ...

Humanity.

She stared round her wildly. There was no sign of the rest house – no sign of the tiny cairn that was the station – no sign, even, of distant hills.

She must have come farther than ever before, so far that all around her there was no discernible landmark.

She didn't, horror upon horror, even know in which direction the rest house lay ...

The hills – surely those distant hills couldn't disappear – but all around on the horizon were low clouds ... Hills? Clouds? One couldn't tell.

She was lost, completely lost ...

No, if she went north – that was right – north.

The sun ...

The sun was directly overhead ... there was no way of telling her direction from the sun ...

She was lost – lost – she would never find the way back ...

Suddenly, frenziedly she began to run.

First in one direction, then, in sudden panic back the other way. She ran to and fro, wildly, desperately.

And she began to cry out – shouting, calling . . .

Help . . .

Help . . .

(They'll never hear me, she thought . . . I'm too far away . . .)

The desert caught up her voice, reduced it to a small bleating cry. Like a sheep, she thought, like a sheep . . .

He findeth his sheep . . .

The Lord is my Shepherd . . .

Rodney – green pastures and the valley in the High Street . . .

Rodney, she called, *help me, help me* . . .

But Rodney was going away up the platform, his shoulders squared, his head thrown back . . . enjoying the thought of a few weeks' freedom . . . feeling, for the moment, young again . . .

He couldn't hear her.

Averil – Averil – wouldn't Averil help her?

I'm your mother, Averil, I've always done everything for you . . .

No, Averil would go quietly out of the room, saying perhaps:

'There isn't really anything I can do . . .'

Tony – Tony would help her.

No, Tony couldn't help her. He was in South Africa.

A long way away . . .

Barbara – Barbara was too ill . . . Barbara had got food poisoning.

Leslie, she thought. Leslie would help me if she could. But Leslie is dead. She suffered and she died . . .

It was no good – there was no one . . .

She began to run again – despairingly, without idea or direction – just running . . .

The sweat was running down her face, down her neck, down her whole body . . .

She thought, This is the end . . .

Christ, she thought . . . *Christ* . . .

Christ would come to her in the desert . . .

Christ would show her the way to the green valley.

. . . Would lead her with the sheep . . .

. . . The lost sheep . . .

. . . The sinner that repented . . .

. . . Through the valley of the shadow . . .

. . . (No shadow – only sun . . .)

. . . Lead kindly light. (But the sun wasn't kindly . . .)

The green valley – the green valley – she must find the green valley . . .

Opening out of the High Street, there in the middle of Crayminster.

Opening out of the desert . . .

Forty days and forty nights.

Only three days gone – so Christ would still be there.

Christ, she prayed, *help me* . . .

Christ . . .

What was that?

Over there – far to the right – that tiny blur upon the horizon!

It *was the rest house*. . . she wasn't lost . . . she was saved . . .

Saved . . .

Her knees gave way – she crumpled down in a heap . . .

Chapter Ten

Joan regained consciousness slowly . . .

She felt very sick and ill . . .

And weak, weak as a child.

But she was saved. The rest house was there. Presently, when she felt a little better, she could get up and walk to it.

In the meantime she would just stay still and think things out. Think them out properly – not pretending any more.

God, after all, had not forsaken her . . .

She had no longer that terrible consciousness of being alone . . .

But I must think, she said to herself. *I must think*. I must get things straight. That is why I'm here – to get things straight . . .

She had got to know, once and for all, just what kind of a woman Joan Scudamore was . . .

That was why she had had to come here, to the desert. This clear, terrible light would show her what she was. Would show her the truth of all the things she hadn't wanted to look at – the things that, really, *she had known all along*.

There had been one clue yesterday. Perhaps she had better start with that. For it had been then, hadn't it, that that first sense of blind panic had swept over her?

She had been reciting poetry – that was how it had begun.

From you have I been absent in the Spring.

That was the line – and it had made her think of Rodney and she had said, 'But it's November now . . .'

Just as Rodney had said that evening, 'But it's October . . .'

The evening of the day that he had sat on Asheldown with Leslie Sherston – the two of them sitting there in silence – with four feet of space between them. And she had thought, hadn't she, that it wasn't very friendly?

But she knew now – and of course she must really have known then – why they sat so far apart.

It was because, wasn't it, they didn't dare to be nearer . . .

Rodney – and Leslie Sherston . . .

Not Myrna Randolph – never Myrna Randolph. She had deliberately encouraged the Myrna Randolph myth in her own mind because she knew there was nothing in it. She had put up Myrna Randolph as a smoke screen so as to hide what was really there.

And partly – be honest now, Joan – partly because it was easier for her to accept Myrna Randolph than Leslie Sherston.

It would hurt her pride less to admit that Rodney had been attracted by Myrna Randolph who was beautiful and the kind of siren who could be supposed to attract any man not gifted with superhuman powers of resistance.

But Leslie Sherston – Leslie who was not even beautiful – who was not young – who was not even well turned out. Leslie with her tired face and her funny one-sided smile. To admit that Rodney could love Leslie – could love her with such passion that he dared not trust himself nearer than four feet – that was what she hated to acknowledge.

That desperate longing, that aching unsatisfied desire – that force of passion that she herself had never known . . .

It had been there between them that day on Asheldown

– and she had felt it – it was because she had felt it that she had hurried away so quickly and so shamefacedly, not admitting to herself for a moment the thing that she really knew . . .

Rodney and Leslie – sitting there silent – not even looking at each other – because they dared not.

Leslie, loving Rodney so desperately, that she wanted to be laid when dead in the town where he lived . . .

Rodney looking down at the marble slab and saying, 'It seems damned silly to think of Leslie Sherston under a cold slab of marble like that.' And the rhododendron bud falling, a scarlet splash.

'Heart's blood,' he had said. 'Heart's blood.'

And then, afterwards, how he had said, 'I'm tired, Joan. I'm tired.' And later, so strangely, 'We can't all be brave . . .'

He had been thinking of Leslie when he said that. Of Leslie and her courage.

'*Courage isn't everything . . .*'

'*Isn't it?*'

And Rodney's nervous breakdown – Leslie's death had been the cause of that.

Lying there peacefully in Cornwall, listening to the gulls, without interest in life, smiling quietly . . .

Tony's scornful boyish voice:

'Don't you know *anything* about Father?'

She hadn't. She hadn't known a thing! Because, quite determinedly, she hadn't wanted to know.

Leslie looking out of the window, explaining why she was going to have Sherston's child.

Rodney, saying as he too looked out of the window, 'Leslie doesn't do things by halves . . .'

What had they seen, these two, as they stood there? Did Leslie see the apple trees and the anemones in her garden? Did Rodney see the tennis court and the goldfish pond? Or did both of them see the pale smiling countryside and the blur of woods on the farther hill that you saw from the summit of Asheldown . . .

Poor Rodney, poor tired Rodney . . .

Rodney with his kind, teasing smile, Rodney saying Poor Little Joan . . . always kind, always affectionate, never failing her . . .

Well, she'd been a good wife to him, hadn't she?

She'd always put his interests first . . .

Wait – had she?

Rodney, his eyes pleading with her . . . sad eyes. Always sad eyes.

Rodney saying, 'How was I to know I'd hate the office so?' looking at her gravely, asking, 'How do you know that I'll be happy?'

Rodney pleading for the life he wanted, the life of a farmer.

Rodney standing at the window of his office watching the cattle on market day.

Rodney talking to Leslie Sherston about dairy herds.

Rodney saying to Averil, 'If a man doesn't do the work he wants to do, he's only half a man.'

That was what she, Joan, had done to Rodney . . .

Anxiously, feverishly, she tried to defend herself against the judgment of her new knowledge.

She had meant it for the best! One had to be practical! There were the children to think of. She hadn't done it from selfish motives.

But the clamour of protestation died down.

Hadn't she been selfish?

Hadn't it been that *she* didn't want to live on a farm herself? She'd wanted her children to have the best things – but what *was* the best? Hadn't Rodney as much right to decide what his children should have as she had?

Hadn't he really the prior right? Wasn't it for a father to choose the life his children should live – the mother to care for their well-being and to follow out, loyally, the father's idea of life?

Life on a farm, Rodney had said, was a good life for children –

Tony would certainly have enjoyed it.

Rodney had seen to it that Tony should not be balked of the kind of life that he wanted.

'I'm not very good,' Rodney had said, 'at forcing people to do things.'

But she, Joan, hadn't scrupled to force Rodney . . .

With a sudden, agonizing pang, Joan thought, But I *love* Rodney. I *love* Rodney. It wasn't that I didn't love him . . .

And that, she saw, with a sudden revealing vision, was just what made it unforgivable.

She loved Rodney and yet she had done this thing to him.

If she had hated him it could be excused.

If she had been indifferent to him, it wouldn't have mattered so much.

But she had loved him, and yet, loving him, she had taken from him his birthright – the right to choose his manner and way of life.

And because of that, because she had used, unscrupulously, her woman's weapons, the child in the cradle, the child that her body was bearing within it – she had taken something from him that he had never recovered. She had taken from him a portion of his manhood.

Because, in his gentleness, he had not fought with her and conquered her, he was so much the less, for all his days on the earth, a man . . .

She thought, Rodney . . . Rodney . . .

She thought, And I can't give it back to him . . . I can't make it up to him . . . I can't do *anything* . . .

But I love him – I do love him . . .

And I love Averil and Tony and Barbara . . .

I always loved them . . .

(But not enough – that was the answer – not enough –)

She thought, Rodney – Rodney, is there *nothing* I can do? Nothing I can say?

From you have I been absent in the Spring.

Yes, she thought, for a long time . . . ever since the spring . . . the spring when we first loved each other . . .

I've stayed where I was – Blanche was right – I'm the girl who left St Anne's. Easy living, lazy thinking, pleased with myself, afraid of anything that might be painful . . .

No *courage* . . .

What can I do, she thought. What can I do?

And she thought, I can go to him. I can say, 'I'm sorry. Forgive me . . .'

Yes, I can say that . . . I can say, 'Forgive me. I didn't know. I simply didn't know . . .'

Joan got up. Her legs felt weak and rather silly.

She walked slowly and painfully – like an old woman.

Walking – walking – one foot – then the other –

Rodney, she thought, Rodney . . .

How ill she felt – how weak . . .

It was a long way – a very long way.

The Indian came running out from the rest house to meet her, his face wreathed in smiles. He waved, gesticulated:

'Good news, Memsahib, good news!'

She stared at him.

'You see? Train come! Train at station. You leave by train tonight.'

The train? The train to take her to Rodney.

('Forgive me, Rodney . . . forgive me . . .')

She heard herself laughing – wildly – unnaturally – the Indian stared and she pulled herself together.

'The train has come,' she said, 'just at the right time . . .'

Chapter Eleven

It was like a dream, Joan thought. Yes, it was like a dream.

Walking through the convolutions of barbed wire – the Arab boy carrying her suitcases and chattering shrilly in Turkish to a big, fat, suspicious looking man who was the Turkish station master.

And there, waiting for her, the familiar sleeping car with the Wagon Lits man in his chocolate uniform leaning out of a window.

Alep-Stamboul on the side of the coach.

The link that bound this resting place in the desert to civilization!

The polite greeting in French, her compartment thrown open, the bed already made with its sheets and its pillow.

Civilization again . . .

Outwardly Joan was once more the quiet, efficient traveller, the same Mrs Scudamore that had left Baghdad less than a week ago. Only Joan herself knew of that astonishing, that almost frightening change that lay behind the façade.

The train, as she had said, had come just at the right moment. Just when those last barriers which she herself had so carefully erected had been swept away in a rising tide of fear and loneliness.

She had had – as others had had in days gone by – a Vision. A vision of *herself*. And although she might seem now the commonplace English traveller, intent on the minor details of travel, her heart and mind were held in that abasement of self reproach that had come to her out there in the silence and the sunlight.

She had answered almost mechanically the Indian's comments and questions.

'Why not Memsahib come back for lunch? Lunch all ready. Very nice lunch. It nearly five o'clock now. Too late lunch. Have tea?'

Yes, she said, she would have tea.

'But where Memsahib go? I look out, not see Memsahib anywhere. Not know which way Memsahib gone.'

She had walked rather far, she said. Farther than usual.

'That not safe. Not safe at all. Memsahib get lost. Not know which way to go. Perhaps walk wrong way.'

Yes, she said, she had lost her way for a time, but luckily she had walked in the right direction. She would have tea now, and then rest. What time did the train go?

'Train go eight-thirty. Sometimes wait for convoy to come in. But no convoy come today. Wadi very bad – lot of water – rush through like that. Whoosh!'

Joan nodded.

'Memsahib look very tired. Memsahib got fever, perhaps?'

No, Joan said, she hadn't got fever – now.

'Memsahib look different.'

Well, she thought, Memsahib *was* different. Perhaps the difference showed in her face. She went to her room and stared into the fly-stained mirror.

Was there any difference? She looked, definitely, older. There were circles under her eyes. Her face was streaked with yellow dust and sweat.

She washed her face, ran a comb through her hair, applied powder and lipstick and looked again.

Yes, there was definitely a difference. Something had gone from the face that stared so earnestly back at her. Something – could it be smugness?

What a horribly smug creature she had been. She felt

still the keen disgust that had come to her out there – the self loathing – the new humility of spirit.

Rodney, she thought, Rodney . . .

Just his name, repeated softly in her thoughts . . .

She held to it as a symbol of her purpose. To tell him everything, not to spare herself. That, she felt, was all that mattered. They would make together, so far as was possible at this late date, a new life. She would say, 'I'm a fool and a failure. Teach me, out of your wisdom, out of your gentleness, the way to live.'

That, and forgiveness. For Rodney had a lot to forgive. And the wonderful thing about Rodney, she realized now, was that he had never hated her. No wonder that Rodney was loved so much – that his children adored him (even Averil, she thought, behind her antagonism, has never stopped loving him), that the servants would do anything to please him, that he had friends everywhere. Rodney, she thought, has never been unkind to anyone in his life . . .

She sighed. She was very tired, and her body ached all over.

She drank her tea and then lay down on her bed until it was time to have dinner and start for the train.

She felt no restlessness now – no fear – no longing for occupation or distraction. There were no more lizards to pop out of holes and frighten her.

She had met herself and recognized herself . . .

Now she only wanted to rest, to lie with an empty, peaceful mind and with always, at the back of that mind, the dim picture of Rodney's kind, dark face . . .

And now she was in the train, had listened to the conductor's voluble account of the accident on the line, had handed over to him her passport and her tickets and had received his assurance that he would wire to Stamboul for fresh reservations on the Simplon Orient Express. She also entrusted him with a wire to be sent from Alep to Rodney. *Journey delayed all well love Joan.*

Rodney would receive it before her original schedule had expired.

So that was all arranged and she had nothing more to do or to think about. She could relax like a tired child.

Five days' peace and quiet whilst the Taurus and Orient Express rushed westwards bringing her each day nearer to Rodney and forgiveness.

They arrived at Alep early the following morning. Until then Joan had been the only passenger, since communications with Iraq were interrupted, but now the train was filled to overflowing. There had been delays, cancellations, confusions in the booking of sleepers. There was a lot of hoarse, excited talking, protests, arguments, disputes – all taking place in different languages.

Joan was travelling first class and on the Taurus Express the first class sleepers were the old double ones.

The door slid back and a tall woman in black came in. Behind her the conductor was reaching down through the window where porters were handing him up cases.

The compartment seemed full of cases – expensive cases stamped with coronets.

The tall woman talked to the attendant in French. She directed him where to put things. At last he withdrew. The woman turned and smiled at Joan, an experienced cosmopolitan smile.

'You are English,' she said.

She spoke with hardly a trace of accent. She had a long, pale, exquisitely mobile face and rather strange light grey eyes. She was, Joan thought, about forty-five.

'I apologize for this early morning intrusion. It is an iniquitously uncivilized hour for a train to leave, and I disturb your repose. Also these carriages are very old-fashioned – on the new ones the compartments are single. But still –' she smiled – and it was a very sweet and almost child-like smile – 'we shall not get too badly on each other's nerves. It is but two days to Stamboul, and I am not too difficult to live with. And if I smoke too much you will tell me. But now I leave you to sleep, I go to the restaurant car that they put on at this moment,' she swayed slightly as a bump indicated the truth of her words, 'and wait there to have breakfast. Again I say how sorry I am you have been disturbed.'

'Oh, that's quite all right,' Joan said. 'One expects these things when travelling.'

'I see you are sympathetic – good – we shall get on together famously.'

She went out and as she drew the door to behind her, Joan heard her being greeted by her friends on the platform with cries of 'Sasha – Sasha' and a voluble burst of conversation in some language that Joan's ear did not recognize.

Joan herself was by now thoroughly awake. She felt rested after her night's sleep. She always slept well in a train. She got up and proceeded to dress. The train drew out of Alep when she had nearly finished her toilet. When she was ready, she went out into the corridor, but first she took a quick look at the labels on her new companion's suitcases.

Princess Hohenbach Salm.

In the restaurant car she found her new acquaintance eating breakfast and conversing with great animation to a small, stout Frenchman.

The princess waved a greeting to her and indicated the seat at her side.

'But you are energetic,' she exclaimed. 'If it was me, I should still lie and sleep. Now, Monsieur Baudier, go on with what you are telling me. It is most interesting.'

The princess talked in French to M. Baudier, in English to Joan, in fluent Turkish to the waiter, and occasionally across the aisle in equally fluent Italian to a rather melancholy looking officer.

Presently the stout Frenchman finished his breakfast and withdrew, bowing politely.

'What a good linguist you are,' said Joan.

The long, pale face smiled – a melancholy smile this time.

'Yes – why not? I am Russian, you see. And I was married to a German, and I have lived much in Italy. I speak eight, nine languages – some well, some not so well. It is a pleasure, do you not think, to converse? All human beings are interesting, and one lives such a short time on this earth! One should exchange ideas – experiences. There is not enough love on the earth, that is what I say. Sasha, my friends say to me, there are people it is impossible to love – Turks, Armenians – Levantines. But I say no. I love them all. *Garçon, l'addition.*'

Joan blinked slightly for the last sentence had been practically joined to the one before it.

The restaurant car attendant came hurrying up respectfully and it was borne in upon Joan that her travelling companion was a person of considerable importance.

All that morning and afternoon they wound across the plains and then climbed slowly up into the Taurus.

Sasha sat in her corner and read and smoked and occasionally made unexpected and sometimes embarrassing remarks. Joan found herself being fascinated by this strange woman who came from a different world and whose mental processes were so totally different from anything she herself had previously come across.

The mingling of the impersonal and the intimate had an odd compelling charm for Joan.

Sasha said to her suddenly:

'You do not read – no? And you do nothing with your

hands. You do not knit. That is not like most English-women. And yet you look most English – yes, you look exactly English.'

Joan smiled.

'I've actually nothing to read. I was held up at Tell Abu Hamid owing to the breakdown on the line, so I got through all the literature I had with me.'

'But you do not mind? You did not feel it necessary to get something at Alep. No, you are content just to sit and look out through the window at the mountains, and yet you do not see them – you look at something that *you yourself see*, is it not so? You experience in your mind some great emotion, or you have passed through one. You have a sorrow? Or a great happiness?'

Joan hesitated, with a slight frown.

Sasha burst out laughing.

'Ah but that is so English. You think it impertinent if I ask the questions that we Russians feel are so natural. It is curious that. If I were to ask you where you had been, to what hotels, and what scenery you had seen, and if you have children and what do they do, and have you travelled much, and do you know a good hairdresser in London – all that you would answer with pleasure. But if I ask something that comes into my mind – have you a sorrow, is your husband faithful – do you sleep much with men – what has been your most beautiful experience in life – are you conscious of the love of God? All those things would make you draw back – affronted – and yet they are much more interesting than the others, nicht wahr?'

'I suppose,' said Joan slowly, 'that we are very reserved as a nation.'

'Yes, yes. One cannot even say to an Englishwoman who has recently been married, are you going to have a baby? That is, one cannot say so across the table at luncheon. No, one has to take her aside, to *whisper* it. And yet if the baby is there, in its cradle, you can say, "How is your baby?"'

'Well – it is rather intimate, isn't it?'

'No, I do not see it. I met the other day a friend I have not seen for many years, a Hungarian. Mitzi, I say to her, you are married – yes, several years now, you have not a baby, why not? She answers me she cannot think why not! For five years, she says she and her husband have tried hard – but oh! how hard they have tried! What, she asks, can she do about it? And, since we are at a luncheon party, everyone there makes a suggestion. Yes, and some of them very practical. Who knows, something may come of it.'

Joan looked stolidly unconvinced.

Yet she felt, suddenly welling up in her, a strong impulse to open her own heart to this friendly, peculiar foreign creature. She wanted, badly, to share with someone the experience that she had been through. She needed, as it were, to assure herself of its reality . . .

She said slowly, 'It is true – I have been through rather an upsetting experience.'

'Ach, yes? What was it? A man?'

'No. No, certainly not.'

'I am glad. It is so often a man – and really in the end it becomes a little boring.'

'I was all alone – at the rest house at Tell Abu Hamid – a horrible place – all flies and tins and rolls of barbed wire, and very gloomy and dark inside.'

'That is necessary because of the heat in summer, but I know what you mean.'

'I had no one to talk to – and I soon finished my books – and I got – I got into a very peculiar state.'

'Yes, yes, that might well be so. It is interesting what you tell me. Go on.'

'I began to find out things – about myself. Things that I had never known before. Or rather things that I *had* known, but had never been willing to recognize. I can't quite explain to you –'

'Oh, but you can. It is quite easy. I shall understand.'

Sasha's interest was so natural, so unassumed, that Joan found herself talking with an astonishing lack of self consciousness. Since to Sasha to talk of one's feelings and one's intimate relationships was perfectly natural, it began to seem natural to Joan also.

She began to talk with less hesitation, describing her uneasiness, her fears, and her final panic.

'I daresay it will seem absurd to you – but I felt that I was completely lost – alone – that God himself had forsaken me –'

'Yes, one has felt that – I have felt it myself. It is very dark, very terrible . . .'

'It was not dark – it was light – blinding light – there was no shelter – no cover – no shadow.'

'We mean the same thing, though. For you it was light that was terrible, because you had hidden so long under cover and in deep shade. But for me it was darkness, not seeing my way, being lost in the night. But the agony is the same – it is the knowledge of one's own nothingness and of being cut off from the love of God.'

Joan said slowly, 'And then – *it happened* – like a miracle. I saw everything. Myself – and what I had been. All my silly pretences and shams fell away. It was like – it was like being born again . . .'

She looked anxiously at the other woman. Sasha bent her head.

'And I knew what I had to do. I had to go home and start again. Build up a new life . . . from the beginning . . .

There was a silence. Sasha was looking at Joan thoughtfully and something in her expression puzzled Joan. She said, with a slight flush:

'Oh, I daresay it sounds very melodramatic and farfetched –'

Sasha interrupted her.

'No, no, you do not understand me. Your experience was real – it has happened to many – to St Paul – to others of the Saints of God – and to ordinary mortals and sinners. It is conversion. It is vision. It is the soul knowing its own bitterness. Yes, it is real all that – it is as real as eating your dinner or brushing your teeth. But I wonder – all the same, I wonder . . .'

'I feel I've been so unkind – done harm to – to someone I love –'

'Yes, yes, you have remorse.'

'And I can hardly wait to get there – to get home, I mean. There is so much I want to say – to tell him.'

'To tell whom? Your husband?'

'Yes. He has been so kind – so patient always. But he has not been happy. I have not made him happy.'

'And you think you will be better able to make him happy now?'

'We can at least have an explanation. He can know how sorry I am. He can help me to – oh, what shall I say?' The words of the Communion service flashed through her mind. 'To lead a new life from now on.'

Sasha said gravely, 'That is what the Saints of God were able to do.'

Joan stared.

'But I – I am not a saint.'

'No. That is what I meant.' Sasha paused, then said with a slight change of tone, 'Forgive me that I should have said that. And perhaps it is not true.'

Joan looked slightly bewildered.

Sasha lit another cigarette and began to smoke violently, staring out of the window.

'I don't know,' said Joan uncertainly, 'why I should tell you all this –'

'But naturally because you wish to tell someone – you

wish to speak of it – it is in your mind and you want to talk of it, that is natural enough.'

'I'm usually very reserved.'

Sasha looked amused.

'And so proud of it like all English people. Oh, you are a very curious race – but very curious. So shamefaced, so embarrassed by your virtues, so ready to admit, to boast of your deficiencies.'

'I think you are exaggerating slightly,' said Joan stiffly.

She felt suddenly very British, very far away from the exotic, pale-faced woman in the opposite corner of the carriage, the woman to whom, a minute or two previously, she had confided a most intimate personal experience.

Joan said in a conventional voice, 'Are you going through on the Simplon Orient?'

'No, I stay a night in Stamboul and then I go to Vienna.' She added carelessly, 'It is possible that I shall die there, but perhaps not.'

'Do you mean –' Joan hesitated, bewildered, 'that you've had a premonition?'

'Ah no,' Sasha burst out laughing. 'No, it it not like that! It is an operation I am going to have there. A very serious operation. Not very often is it that it succeeds. But they are good surgeons in Vienna. This one to whom I am going – he is very clever – a Jew. I have always said it would be stupid to annihilate all the Jews in Europe. They are clever doctors and surgeons, yes, and they are clever artistically too.'

'Oh dear,' said Joan. 'I am so sorry.'

'Because I may be going to die? But what does it matter? One has to die some time. And I may not die. I have the idea, if I live, that I will enter a convent I know of – a very strict order. One never speaks – it is perpetual meditation and prayer.'

Joan's imagination failed to conceive of a Sasha perpetually silent and meditating.

Sasha went on gravely, 'There will be much prayer needed soon – when the war comes.'

'*War*?' Joan stared.

Sasha nodded her head.

'But yes, certainly war is coming. Next year, or the year after.'

'Really,' said Joan. 'I think you are mistaken.'

'No, no. I have friends who are very well informed and they have told me so. It is all decided.'

'But war where – against whom?'

'War everywhere. Every nation will be drawn in. My friends think that Germany will win quite soon, but I – I do not agree. Unless they can win very very quickly indeed. You see, I know many English and Americans and I know what they are like.'

'Surely,' said Joan, 'nobody really wants war.'

She spoke incredulously.

'For what else does the Hitler Youth movement exist?'

Joan said earnestly, 'But I have friends who have been in Germany a good deal, and they think that there is a lot to be said for the Nazi movement.'

'Oh la la,' cried Sasha. 'See if they say that in three years' time.'

Then she leaned forward as the train drew slowly to a standstill.

'See, we have come to the Cilician Gates. It is beautiful, is it not? Let us get out.'

They got out of the train and stood looking down through the great gap in the mountain chain to the blue, hazy plains beneath . . .

It was close on sunset and the air was exquisitely cool and still.

Joan thought: How beautiful . . .

She wished Rodney was here to see it with her.

Chapter Twelve

Victoria . . .

Joan felt her heart beating with sudden excitement.

It was good to be home.

She felt, just for a moment, as though she had never been away. England, her own country. Nice English porters . . . A not so nice, but very English, foggy day!

Not romantic, not beautiful, just dear old Victoria station just the same as ever, looking just the same, smelling just the same!

Oh, thought Joan, I'm *glad* to be back.

Such a long, weary journey, across Turkey and Bulgaria and Yugoslavia and Italy and France. Customs officers, and passport examinations. All the different uniforms, all the different languages. She was tired – yes, definitely tired – of foreigners. Even that extraordinary Russian woman who had travelled with her from Alep to Stamboul had got rather tiresome in the end. She had been interesting – indeed quite exciting – to begin with, simply because she was so different. But by the time they had been running down beside the Sea of Marmora to Haidar Pacha, Joan had been definitely looking forward to their parting. For one thing it was embarrassing to remember how freely, she, Joan, had talked about her own private affairs to a complete stranger. And for another – well, it was difficult to put it into words – but something about her had made Joan feel definitely *provincial*. Not a very pleasant feeling. It had been no good to say to herself that she hoped she, Joan, was as good as anybody! She didn't really think so. She felt uneasily conscious that

Sasha, for all her friendliness, was an aristocrat whilst she herself was middle class, the unimportant wife of a country solicitor. Very stupid, of course, to feel like that . . .

But anyway all that was over now. She was home again, back on her native soil.

There was no one to meet her for she had sent no further wire to Rodney to tell him when she was arriving.

She had had a strong feeling that she wanted to meet Rodney in their own house. She wanted to be able to start straight away on her confession without pause or delay. It would be easier so, she thought.

You couldn't very well ask a surprised husband for forgiveness on the platform at Victoria!

Certainly not on the arrival platform, with its hurrying mob of people, and the Customs sheds at the end.

No, she would spend the night quietly at the Grosvenor and go down to Crayminster tomorrow.

Should she, she wondered, try and see Averil first? She could ring Averil up from the hotel.

Yes, she decided. She might do that.

She had only hand luggage with her and as it had already been examined at Dover, she was able to go with her porter straight to the hotel.

She had a bath and dressed and then rang up Averil. Fortunately Averil was at home.

'Mother? I'd no idea you were back.'

'I arrived this afternoon.'

'Is Father up in London?'

'No. I didn't tell him when I was arriving. He might have come up to meet me – and that would be a pity if he's busy – tiring for him.'

She thought that she heard a faint note of surprise in Averil's voice as she said:

'Yes – I think you were right. He's been very busy lately.'

'Have you seen much of him?'

'No. He was up in London for the day about three weeks ago and we had lunch together. What about this evening, Mother? Would you like to come out and have dinner somewhere?'

'I'd rather you came here, darling, if you don't mind. I'm a little tired with travelling.'

'I expect you must be. All right, I'll come round.'

'Won't Edward come with you?'

'He's got a business dinner tonight.'

Joan put down the receiver. Her heart was beating a little faster than usual. She thought, Averil – my Averil . . .

How cool and liquid Averil's voice was . . . calm, detached, impersonal.

Half an hour later they telephoned up that Mrs Harrison-Wilmott was there and Joan went down.

Mother and daughter greeted each other with English reserve. Averil looked well, Joan thought. She was not quite so thin. Joan felt a faint thrill of pride as she went with her daughter into the dining-room. Averil was really very lovely, so delicate and distinguished looking.

They sat down at a table and Joan got a momentary shock as she met her daughter's eyes.

They were so cool and uninterested . . .

Averil, like Victoria Station, had not changed.

It's I who have changed, thought Joan, but Averil doesn't know that.

Averil asked about Barbara and about Baghdad. Joan recounted various incidents of her journey home. Somehow or other, their talk was rather difficult. It did not seem to flow. Averil's inquiries after Barbara were almost perfunctory. It really seemed as though she had an inkling that more pertinent questions might be indiscreet. But Averil couldn't know anything of the truth. It was just her usual delicate, incurious attitude.

The truth, Joan thought suddenly, *how do I know it*

is the truth? Mightn't it, just possibly, be all imagination on her part? After all, there was no concrete evidence . . .

She rejected the idea, but the mere passing of it through her head had given her a shock. Supposing she was one of those people who imagined things . . .

Averil was saying in her cool voice, 'Edward has got it into his head that there's bound to be war with Germany one day.'

Joan roused herself.

'That's what a woman on the train said. She seemed quite certain about it. She was rather an important person, and she really seemed to know what she was talking about. I can't believe it. Hitler would never *dare* to go to war.'

Averil said thoughtfully, 'Oh, I don't know . . .'

'Nobody *wants* war, darling.'

'Well, people sometimes get what they don't want.'

Joan said decidedly, 'I think all this talk of it is very dangerous. It puts ideas into people's heads.'

Averil smiled.

They continued to talk in rather a desultory fashion. After dinner, Joan yawned, and Averil said she wouldn't stay and keep her up – she must be tired.

Joan said, Yes, she was rather tired.

On the following day Joan did a little shopping in the morning and caught the 2.30 train to Crayminster. That would get her there just after four o'clock. She would be waiting for Rodney when he came home at tea time from the office . . .

She looked out of the carriage window with appreciation. Nothing much in the way of scenery to see this time of year – bare trees, a faint, misty rain falling – but how natural, how homelike. Baghdad with its crowded bazaars, its brilliant blue domed and golden mosques, was far away – unreal – it might never have happened. That long, fantastic journey, the plains of Anatolia, the snows and mountain scenery of the Taurus, the high, bare plains – the long descent through mountain gorges to the Bosphorus, Stamboul with its minarets, the funny ox wagons of the Balkans – Italy with the blue Adriatic Sea glistening as they left Trieste – Switzerland and the Alps in the darkening light – a panorama of different sights and scenes – and all ending in this – this journey home through the quiet winter countryside . . .

I might never have been away, thought Joan. I *might never have been away . . .*

She felt confused, unable to co-ordinate her thoughts clearly. Seeing Averil last night had upset her – Averil's cool eyes looking at her, calm, incurious. *Averil,* she thought, *hadn't seen any difference in her*. Well, after all, why should Averil see a difference?

It wasn't her physical appearance that had changed.

She said very softly to herself, '*Rodney . . .*'

The glow came back – the sorrow – the yearning for love and forgiveness . . .

She thought, It's all true . . . I *am* beginning a new life . . .

She took a taxi up from the station. Agnes opened the door and displayed a flattering surprise and pleasure.

The Master, Agnes said, *would* be pleased.

Joan went up to her bedroom, took off her hat, and came down again. The room looked a little bare, but that was because it had no flowers in it.

I must cut some laurel tomorrow, she thought, and get some carnations from the shop at the corner.

She walked about the room feeling nervous and excited.

Should she tell Rodney what she had guessed about Barbara? Supposing that, after all –

Of course it wasn't true! She had *imagined* the whole thing. Imagined it all because of what that stupid woman Blanche Haggard – no, Blanche Donovan – had said.

Really, Blanche had looked too terrible – so old and coarse.

Joan put her hand to her head. She felt as though, within her brain, was a kaleidoscope. She had had a kaleidoscope as a child and loved it, had held her breath as all the coloured pieces whirled and revolved, before settling down into a pattern . . .

What *had* been the matter with her?

That horrible rest house place and that very odd experience she had had in the desert . . . She had imagined all sorts of unpleasant things – that her children didn't like her – that Rodney had loved Leslie Sherston (of course he hadn't – what an idea! Poor Leslie). And she had even been regretful because she had persuaded Rodney out of that extraordinary fancy of his to take up farming. Really, she had been very sensible and far-seeing . . .

Oh dear, why was she so confused? All those things she had been thinking and believing – such unpleasant things . . .

Were they actually true? Or weren't they? *She didn't want them to be true.*

She'd got to decide – she'd got to decide . . .

What had she got to decide?

The sun – thought Joan – the sun was very hot. The sun does give you hallucinations . . .

Running in the desert . . . falling on her hands and knees . . . praying . . .

Was *that* real?

Or was *this*?

Madness – absolute madness the things she had been believing. How comfortable, how pleasant to come home to England and feel you had never been away. That everything was just the same as you had always thought it was . . .

And *of course* everything was just the same.

A kaleidoscope whirling . . . whirling . . .

Settling presently into one pattern or the other.

Rodney, forgive me – I didn't know . . .

Rodney, here I am. I've come home!

Which pattern? *Which*? She'd got to choose.

She heard the sound of the front door opening – a sound she knew so well – so very well . . .

Rodney was coming.

Which pattern? Which pattern? *Quick*!

The door opened. Rodney came in. He stopped, surprised.

Joan came quickly forward. She didn't look at once at his face. *Give him a moment*, she thought, *give him a moment . . .*

Then she said gaily, '*Here I am, Rodney . . . I've come home . . .*'

Epilogue

Rodney Scudamore sat in the small, low-backed chair while his wife poured out tea, and clanked the teaspoons, and chattered brightly about how nice it was to be home again and how delightful it was to find everything exactly the same and that Rodney wouldn't believe how wonderful it was to be back in England again, and back in Crayminster, and back in her own home!

On the windowpane a big bluebottle, deceived by the unusual warmth of the early November day, buzzed importantly up and down the glass.

Buzz, buzz, buzz, went the bluebottle.

Tinkle, tinkle, tinkle went Joan Scudamore's voice.

Rodney sat smiling and nodding his head.

Noises, he thought, noises . . .

Meaning everything to some people, and nothing at all to others.

He had been mistaken, he decided, in thinking that there was something wrong with Joan when she first arrived. There was nothing wrong with Joan. She was just the same as usual. Everything was just the same as usual.

Presently Joan went upstairs to see to her unpacking, and Rodney went across the hall to his study where he had brought some work home from the office.

But first he unlocked the small top right-hand drawer of his desk and took out Barbara's letter. It had come by Air Mail and had been sent off a few days before Joan's departure from Baghdad.

It was a long closely written letter and he knew it now

almost by heart. Nevertheless, he read it through again, dwelling a little on the last page.

– So now I have told you everything, darling Dads. I daresay you guessed most of it already. You needn't worry about me. I do realize just what a criminal, wicked little fool I have been. Remember, Mother knows *nothing*. It wasn't too easy keeping it all from her, but Dr McQueen played up like a trump and William was wonderful. I really don't know what I should have done without him – he was always there, ready to fend Mother off, if things got difficult. I felt pretty desperate when she wired she was coming out. I know you must have tried to stop her, darling, and that she just wouldn't be stopped – and I suppose it was really rather sweet of her in a way – only of course she *had* to rearrange our whole lives for us and it was simply maddening, and I felt too weak to struggle much! I'm only just beginning to feel that Mopsy is my own again! She is sweet. I wish you could see her. Did you like us when we were babies, or only later? Darling Dads, I'm so glad I had you for a father. Don't worry about me. I'm all right now.

Your loving Babs.

Rodney hesitated a moment, holding the letter. He would have liked to have kept it. It meant a great deal to him – that written declaration of his daughter's faith and trust in him.

But in the exercise of his profession he had seen, only too often, the dangers of kept letters. If he were to die suddenly Joan would go through his papers and come across it, and it would cause her needless pain. No need for her to be hurt and dismayed. Let her remain happy and secure in the bright, confident world that she had made for herself.

He went across the room and dropped Barbara's letter

into the fire. Yes, he thought, she would be all right now. They would all be all right. It was for Barbara he had feared most – with her unbalanced deeply emotional temperament. Well, the crisis had come and she had escaped, not unscathed, but alive. And already she was realizing that Mopsy and Bill were truly her world. A good fellow, Bill Wray. Rodney hoped that he hadn't suffered too much.

Yes, Barbara would be all right. And Tony was all right in his orange groves in Rhodesia – a long way away, but all right – and that young wife of his sounded the right kind of girl. Nothing had ever hurt Tony much – perhaps it never would. He had that sunny type of mind.

And Averil was all right too. As always, when he thought of Averil, it was pride he felt, not pity. Averil with her dry legal mind, and her passion for understatement. Averil, with her cool, sarcastic tongue. So rock-like, so staunch, so strangely unlike the name they had given her.

He had fought Averil, fought her and vanquished her with the only weapons her disdainful mind would recognize, weapons that he himself had found it distasteful to use. Cold reasons, logical reasons, pitiless reasons – she had accepted those.

But had she forgiven him? He thought not. But it didn't matter. If he had destroyed her love for him, he had retained and enhanced her respect – and in the end, he thought, to a mind like hers and to her flawless rectitude, it is respect that counts.

On the eve of her wedding day, speaking to his best-loved child across the great gulf that now separated them, he had said:

'I hope you will be happy.'

And she had answered quietly, 'I shall try to be happy.'

That was Averil – no heroics, no dwelling on the past – no self-pity. A disciplined acceptance of life – and the ability to live it without help from others.

He thought, They're out of my hands now, the three of them.

Rodney pushed back the papers on his desk and came over to sit in the chair on the right of the fireplace. He took with him the Massingham lease and sighing slightly started to read it over.

> 'The Landlord lets and the tenant takes all that farm-house buildings lands and hereditaments situate at . . .' He read on and turned the page. 'not to take more than two white straw crops of corn from any part of the arable lands without a summer fallow (a crop of turnips and rape sown on land well cleaned and manured and eaten on such land with sheep to be considered equivalent to a fallow) and . . .'

His hand relaxed and his eyes wandered to the empty chair opposite.

That was where Leslie had sat when he argued with her about the children and the undesirability of their coming in contact with Sherston. She ought, he had said, to consider the children.

She *had* considered them, she said – and after all, he *was* their father.

A father who had been in prison, he said – an ex-jailbird – public opinion – ostracism – cutting them off from their normal social existence – penalizing them unfairly. She ought, he said, to think of all that. Children, he said, should not have their youth clouded. They should start fair.

And she had said, 'That's just it. He *is* their father. It isn't so much that *they* belong to *him* as that *he* belongs to *them*. I can wish, of course, that they'd had a different kind of father – but it isn't so.'

And she had said, 'What kind of a start in life would it be – to begin by running away from what's there?'

Well, he saw her idea, of course. But it didn't agree

with his ideas. He'd always wanted to give his children the best of things – indeed, that was what he and Joan had done. The best schools, the sunniest rooms in the house – they'd practised small economies themselves to make that possible.

But in their case there had never been any moral problem. There had been no disgrace, no dark shadow, no failure, despair and anguish, no question of that kind when it would have been necessary to say, 'Shall we shield them? Or let them share?'

And it was Leslie's idea, he saw, that they should share. She, although she loved them, would not shrink from placing a portion of her burden on those small, untrained backs. Not selfishly, not to ease her own load, but because she did not want to deny them even the smallest, most unendurable part of reality.

Well, he thought that she was wrong. But he admitted, as he had always admitted, her courage. It went beyond courage for herself. She had courage for those she loved.

She remembered Joan saying that autumn day as he went to the office:

'Courage? Oh yes, but courage isn't everything?'

And he had said, 'Isn't it?'

Leslie sitting there in his chair, with her left eyebrow going slightly up and her right eyebrow down and with the little twist at the right-hand corner of her mouth and her head against the faded blue cushion that made her hair look – somehow – green.

He remembered his voice, slightly surprised, saying:

'Your hair's not brown. It's *green*.'

It was the only personal thing he'd ever said to her. He'd never thought, very much, what she looked like. Tired, he knew, and ill – and yet, withal, *strong* – yes, physically strong. He had thought once, incongruously, She could sling a sack of potatoes over her shoulder just like a man.

Not a very romantic thought and there wasn't, really, anything very romantic that he could remember about her. The right shoulder higher than the left, the left eyebrow going up and the right down, the little twist at the corner of her mouth when she smiled, the brown hair that looked green against a faded blue cushion.

Not much, he thought, for love to feed on. And what was love? In Heaven's name, what *was* love? The peace and content that he'd felt to see her sitting there, in his chair, her head green against the blue cushion. The way she had said suddenly, 'You know, I've been thinking about Copernicus –'

Copernicus? Why in Heaven's name, Copernicus? A monk with an idea – with a vision of a differently shaped world – and who was cunning and adroit enough to compromise with the powers of the world and to write his faith in such a form as would pass muster.

Why should Leslie, with her husband in prison, and her living to earn and her children to worry about, sit there running a hand through her hair and say, 'I've been thinking about Copernicus'?

Yet because of that, for always, at the mention of Copernicus his own heart would miss a beat, and up there, on the wall, he had hung an old engraving of the monk, to say to him, '*Leslie*.'

He thought, I should at least have told her that I loved her. I might have said so – once.

But had there been any need? That day on Asheldown – sitting there in the October sunlight. He and she together – together and apart. The agony and the desperate longing. Four feet of space between them – four feet because there couldn't safely be less. She had understood that. She must have understood that. He thought confusedly, That space between us – like an electric field – charged with longing.

They had not looked at each other. He had looked

down over the ploughland and the farm, with the distant faint sound of the tractor and the pale purple of the upturned earth. And Leslie had looked beyond the farmland to the woods.

Like two people gazing at a promised land to which they could not enter in. He thought, I should have told her that I loved her then.

But neither of them had said anything – except just that once when Leslie had murmured, '*And thy eternal summer shall not fade*.'

Just that. One hackneyed line of quotation. And he didn't even know what she had meant by it.

Or perhaps he did. Yes, perhaps he did.

The chair cushion had faded. And Leslie's face. He couldn't remember her face clearly, only that queer twist of the mouth.

And yet for the last six weeks she had sat there every day and talked to him. Just fantasy, of course. He had invented a pseudo Leslie, and put her there in the chair, and put words into her mouth. He had made her say what he wanted her to say, and she had been obedient, but her mouth had curved upwards at the side as though she had laughed at what he was doing to her.

It had been, he thought, a very happy six weeks. He'd been able to see Watkins and Mills and there had been that jolly evening with Hargrave Taylor – just a few friends and not too many of them. That pleasant tramp across the hills on Sunday. The servants had given him very good meals and he'd eaten them as slowly as he liked, with a book propped up against the soda water syphon. Some work to finish sometimes after dinner, and then a pipe and finally, just in case he might feel lonely, false Leslie arranged in her chair to keep him company.

False Leslie, yes, but hadn't there been, somewhere, not very far away, real Leslie?

And thy eternal summer shall not fade.

He looked down again at the lease.

'. . . and shall in all respects cultivate the said farm in due and regular course of good husbandry.'

He thought wonderingly, I'm really quite a good lawyer.

And then, without wonder (and without much interest), '*I'm successful.*'

Farming, he thought, was a difficult, heartbreaking business.

'My God, though,' he thought, 'I'm tired.'

He hadn't felt so tired for a long time.

The door opened and Joan came in.

'Oh, Rodney – you can't read that without the light on.'

She rustled across behind him and turned the light on. He smiled and thanked her.

'You're so stupid, darling, to sit here ruining your eyes when all you've got to do is just to turn a switch.'

She added affectionately as she sat down, 'I don't know what you'd do without me.'

'Get into all sort of bad habits.'

His smile was teasing, kindly.

'Do you remember,' Joan went on, 'when you suddenly got an idea you wanted to turn down Uncle Henry's offer and take up farming instead?'

'Yes, I remember.'

'Aren't you glad now I wouldn't let you?'

He looked at her, admiring her eager competence, the youthful poise of her neck, her smooth, pretty, unlined face. Cheerful, confident, affectionate. He thought, Joan's been a very good wife to me.

He said quietly, 'Yes, I'm glad.'

Joan said, 'We all get impractical ideas sometimes.'

'Even you?'

He said it teasingly, but was surprised to see her frown.

An expression passed over her face like a ripple across smooth water.

'One gets nervy sometimes – morbid.'

He was still more surprised. He could not imagine Joan nervy or morbid. Changing the subject he said:

'You know I quite envy you your journey out East.'

'Yes, it was interesting. But I shouldn't like to have to live in a place like Baghdad.'

Rodney said thoughtfully, 'I'd like to know what the desert is like. It must be rather wonderful – emptiness and a clear strong light. It's the idea of the light that fascinates me. To see clearly –'

Joan interrupted him. She said vehemently, 'It's hateful – hateful – just arid nothingness!'

She looked round the room with a sharp, nervous glance. Rather, he thought, like an animal that wants to escape.

Her brow cleared. She said, 'That cushion's dreadfully old and faded. I must get a new one for that chair.'

He made a sharp instinctive gesture, then checked himself.

After all, why not? A cushion was faded. Leslie Adeline Sherston was in the churchyard under a marble slab. The firm of Alderman, Scudamore and Witney was forging ahead. Farmer Hoddesdon was trying to raise another mortgage.

Joan was walking round the room, testing a ledge for dust, replacing a book in the bookshelf, moving the ornaments on the mantelpiece. It was true that in the last six weeks the room had acquired an untidy, shabby appearance.

Rodney murmured to himself softly, 'The holidays are over.'

'What?' she whirled round on him. 'What did you say?'

He blinked at her disarmingly. 'Did I say anything?'

'I thought you said "the holidays are over." You must

have dropped off and been dreaming – about the children going back to school.'

'Yes,' said Rodney, 'I must have been dreaming.'

She stood looking at him doubtfully. Then she straightened a picture on the wall.

'What's this? It's new, isn't it?'

'Yes. I picked it up at Hartley's sale.'

'Oh,' Joan eyed it doubtfully. 'Copernicus? Is it valuable?'

'I've no idea,' said Rodney. He repeated thoughtfully, 'I've no idea at all . . .'

What was valuable, what was not? Was there such a thing as remembrance?

'*You know, I've been thinking about Copernicus . . .*'

Leslie, with her shifty jail bird of a husband – drunkenness, poverty, illness, death.

'*Poor Mrs Sherston, such a sad life.*'

But, he thought, Leslie wasn't sad. She walked through disillusionment and poverty and illness like a man walks through bogs and over plough and across rivers, cheerfully and impatiently, to get to wherever it is he is going . . .

He looked thoughtfully at his wife out of tired but kindly eyes.

So bright and efficient and busy, so pleased and successful. He thought, She doesn't look a day over twenty-eight.

And suddenly a vast upwelling rush of pity swept over him.

He said with intense feeling, 'Poor little Joan.'

She stared at him. She said, 'Why poor? And I'm little.'

He said in his old teasing voice, '*Here am I, little Joan. If nobody's with me I'm all alone.*'

She came to him with a sudden rush, almost breathing, she said:

'I'm not alone. I'm not alone. I've got *you*.'

'Yes,' said Rodney. 'You've got me.'

But he knew as he said it that it wasn't true. He thought:

You are alone and you always will be. But, please God, you'll never know it.